YOUR NEIGHBOUR'S TABLE

Books by Gu Byeong-mo, which are available in English:

The Old Woman with the Knife (Canongate, 2022)

Forthcoming from Wildfire:

The Wizard's Bakery (August 2025)

YOUR NEIGHBOUR'S TABLE

Gu Byeong-mo

Translated by Chi-young Kim

WILDFIRE

Originally published in South Korea as 네 이웃의 식탁 by Minumsa Publishing Co. Ltd in 2018.

This English language edition is published in 2024 by WILDFIRE, an imprint of HEADLINE PUBLISHING GROUP, in arrangement with Minumsa Publishing Co. Ltd., and Casanovas & Lynch Literary Agency

1

Cataloguing in Publication Data is available from the British Library

Trade Paperback ISBN 978 1 0354 1647 9

Offset in 13.8/18.2pt Bembo MT Pro by Jouve (UK), Milton Keynes

Printed and bound in Great Britain by Clays Ltd, Elcograf S.p.A.

Headline's policy is to use papers that are natural, renewable and recyclable products and made from wood grown in well-managed forests and other controlled sources. The logging and manufacturing processes are expected to conform to the environmental regulations of the country of origin.

HEADLINE PUBLISHING GROUP
An Hachette UK Company
Carmelite House
50 Victoria Embankment
London EC4Y 0DZ

www.headline.co.uk
www.hachette.co.uk

YOUR NEIGHBOUR'S TABLE

Jeon Euno and **Seo Yojin**
Jeon Siyul (age six)

Sin Jaegang and **Hong Danhui**
Sin Jeongmok (age five)
Sin Jeonghyeop (age three)

Go Yeosan and **Gang Gyowon**
Go Ubin (age four)
Go Seah (infant)

Son Sangnak and **Jo Hyonae**
Son Darim (seventeen months)

The backyard table was big enough to seat approximately sixteen adults, assuming you didn't mind brushing elbows with your neighbors each time you reached over to grab a napkin or a cup, big enough to squeeze in an additional half dozen kids if you packed in tight and didn't mind someone else breathing on you. This handcrafted table was too heavy even for four or five brawny men to pick up and move—its smooth tabletop was coated in varnish so glossy that you could almost see your face in it, its hefty corners were roughly hewn, and its legs, five thick pillars practically drilled into the ground, showed off the bumpy musculature of the wood used to make them. It was unknown who among the architects of this small apartment building had thought to install something like this in the backyard. But the table obviously wasn't an afterthought; a regular person with an ordinary job would never be able to afford such an extravagant custom piece.

With only seven adults and six kids, three of whom were on their dads' laps, there was plenty of room around the table right now. It would become more challenging to accommodate everyone once all twelve units were fully occupied, but Yojin figured the families would rarely gather to eat as a group.

"All right, has everyone poured themselves a glass of wine?" Sin Jaegang, who had dashed out to greet Yojin's family the moment their moving truck extended its ladder to reach their windowsill, stood up. "Welcome, Mr. Jeon Euno, Ms. Seo Yojin, and six-year-old Miss Jeon Siyul!"

"Welcome!"

"Nice to meet you!"

All the adults got up and raised their glasses, bowing in greeting, except for the dads with kids on their laps, who managed only to lift their arms. They clinked glasses and nodded at their neighbors across the table, and the kids imitated them, holding up their biodegradable plastic cups of tangerine juice before taking a gulp. Earlier, Jaegang had introduced Yojin and Euno to the other residents: "Calling someone So-and-so's mom or So-and-so's dad is no fun at all, don't you think? Here we prefer to be called by our given names." Now, reeling from the strangeness of hearing someone uttering her name outside of the doctor's or a government office, Yojin murmured her own name like an immigrant savoring the rarely used pronunciation of her native language, then ran her tongue across her gums.

Still holding his sleeping child awkwardly, Go Yeosan turned toward Euno. "We thought you'd be tired after moving in, so we figured we'd just do some snacks and refreshments. I'm afraid it's not the most enthusiastic welcome."

Euno's expression was grateful as he batted Yeosan's words away. "Not at all. It's best to keep things simple. We aren't short-term guests or people who need to be wined and dined. We're just..." Here, he clinked his glass with Yeosan's without finishing his sentence; he figured he would come across as bristly, even if his tone were pleasant, if he said, *We're just the three newest residents joining this communal housing pilot program.*

The clinking of dishware, the murmur of conversation, and the whining of children hung in the early evening air. Gang Gyowon, Yeosan's wife, had pushed her glass away and was trying to feed their four-year-old son a late lunch. Even her flashes of irritation seemed to embody the pleasure of an affection-filled afternoon. Nobody coming across this scene would want to ruin this picture, this wholesome moment between mother and son. Living communally meant recasting noise as background music and messy scenes as frameworthy.

"Yojin-ssi, did you put the sheet of paper I gave you somewhere safe?" asked Hong Danhui, Jaegang's wife.

Yojin had only a faint recollection of accepting something from Danhui during the chaos of the move, but didn't let on that she was flustered.

"It's nothing too important, just some house rules," Danhui explained. "I wrote down the recycling days and things like that, so all you have to do is follow the schedule."

Realizing what Danhui was talking about, Yojin let out a sigh of relief like a bride who'd finished bowing to her new in-laws during the pyebaek ceremony.

"Oh, that's right. We're not fully unpacked yet, so I just stuck it on the fridge. I'll give it a read as soon as I get home."

"Tomorrow's Sunday, so you have plenty of time. Anyway, Sangnak-ssi, is Hyonae-ssi super busy these days?"

Son Sangnak gave a brief nod and, preoccupied with giving his drowsy baby a bottle, muttered, "Oh, she's always busy."

Eight adults should have been present to account for every couple, but Yojin realized that Sangnak's wife wasn't there. *Oh, she's always busy.* It was an honest if terse response, possibly even insincere depending on how you looked at it. Maybe his answer was an effort to curtail the line of questioning, but Danhui added another weighted question.

"Even if she's on deadline, how hard is it to come out for a quick hello? We have a new family moving in. And you had to bring Darim out on your own."

"It's just that she barely managed to meet her deadline. She passed out right after. She didn't sleep at all the last three nights, so she won't wake up even if someone tried to haul her away right now."

"Well. I guess there's nothing we can do if she's sleeping. Yojin-ssi, you're not upset, are you?"

"Of course not!" Yojin waved away the suggestion. "Everyone has stuff going on, and we're no VIPs."

As Euno had said earlier, they weren't guests and there was no need for formalities. Their relationship with their neighbors would be casual. In any other apartment building, they'd share a passing smile at most, and even now, having become a defined group of sorts due to the circumstances of their housing situation, knowing one another's names was more than enough. But the way Danhui kept needling Sangnak felt loaded; Yojin wasn't unaware of how the demand of "a quick hello," such small, seemingly trivial moments, could pile up and harden, encroaching on one's life. There were plenty of people who found it impossible to stand up for a quick greeting and plenty of situations in which doing the simplest thing for someone else was impractical.

On closer examination, Danhui, who appeared to be a few years older than Yojin, seemed like the type of person who would lead a women's association, driven by a preternaturally outgoing personality and love for appraising and organizing various matters. Yojin found it curious that someone like her had decided to live in such a remote village. This was the kind of place you'd move to in order to cut social ties, the kind of place where you measured quality of life by clean air and clean water.

"Now that your family has moved in, it finally feels like a community," Danhui said, her tone friendly. "I mean, it wasn't like we were lonely by ourselves or anything. But since Hyonae-ssi is some kind of free-lancer and works at night and sleeps during the day, it felt like there were just two of us women. It's great that we now have another! Let's have tea after we send our husbands to work and get to know each other."

Yojin merely smiled, figuring she didn't need to correct Danhui right this second, but Euno spoke up. "Actually, she's the one who goes to work while I stay home with Siyul."

"Oh?"

Euno chuckled. "I'm pretty unimpressive, so she's the one who works outside the home."

Euno enjoyed using self-deprecation as a way to praise Yojin, but this habit of his sometimes made her feel awful, even though she knew he was trying to be nice. She didn't want him to cut himself down to boost her up—nothing sparkled in the light of comparative put-downs, and, more importantly, none of it ever sounded like a compliment to her.

"Oh… I see. So Yojin-ssi was making more, and that's why Euno-ssi decided to stay home."

"Well, not exactly," Yojin said vaguely, not wanting to get into how her husband was moping around like a bum after several of his films had fallen through, at least not during their first encounter with the neighbors. But she found herself worrying that Danhui might keep asking questions the way she had with Sangnak earlier, unable—or refusing—to read between the lines.

"Then Yojin-ssi—well, I'm not sure if I should ask you this when the unemployment rate is so high and it's so hard to get a permanent position, I mean, it's really hard for everyone right now—where do you work?"

Thankfully, the interrogation at least moved toward Yojin instead of staying on Euno. Though she didn't know why someone would say she wasn't sure if she should ask a question and then go ahead and ask it anyway, Yojin had at least expected this one, a question always added on like a surcharge whenever people learned that her husband stayed home and she went to work.

Euno beat her to it once again. "She works at a pharmacy. It's right next to a neighborhood pediatrician's office."

"Euno-ssi, you're quite the spokesperson! You're not letting your wife speak. So, a pharmacist! How impressive."

Jaegang jumped in. "Euno-ssi, you must be one of those lucky fellows we've heard tell of! A man whose wife provides for him!"

Yojin swallowed a mouthful of bitter, tart wine. "No, I—" Yojin was reluctant to divulge too much about her personal life, but she was a firm believer in the power of clarity. It helped quash potential misunderstandings. "I'm just the cashier."

Yojin was an assistant to her pharmacist cousin, who had opened her own pharmacy. Her main duties were filling the scrips patients brought from the medical building next door, handing over herbal teas and nutritional tonics customers sought, and ringing up organic grain snacks and kids' vitamin drinks as well as bandages, masks, and other personal hygiene products at the counter. She also swept and mopped inside and out, cleaned the medicine cabinets and the shelves, sorted the trash, kept up with the inventory, checked manufacture dates, removed expired medications and reorganized them.

She wasn't a pharmacist or a specialist in medicine and didn't have a wealth of pharmaceutical knowledge, but she'd still memorized the active ingredients of commonly requested medications just in case, and, as a mother, learned the differences and the alternating dosages of Tylenol and ibuprofen; some of the tasks she handled technically violated the Pharmaceutical Affairs Act, but patients and guardians rarely took issue with her involvement, especially when there were hundreds of scrips to be filled in a day. Most importantly, she was efficient with the computer, and though it made her blood run cold to imagine misreading the name of a medication she gave a patient, she'd never made a grave mistake like that; she didn't even need to type in the correct spelling or chemical formula of a medication since she used a pharmacy-exclusive system that handled most of the process with a beep of the POS terminal.

If she were to amend any part of what Euno said, it would be the leisurely descriptor of "a neighborhood pediatrician's office." As the pharmacy was in a bustling neighborhood next to a medical building filled with all kinds of practices, Yojin didn't even have time for a lunch break on Mondays or on a day after a holiday. Still, they had it better than the pharmacy housed inside the medical building, which was busy enough to employ three pharmacists; she and her cousin could at least take breaks from time to time.

"Oh... I see." Danhui was now embarrassed, and as she trailed off, Gyowon jumped in.

"What's wrong with working as a cashier? All that matters is working hard and making an honest living."

"Of course not, there's nothing wrong with it!" Danhui recovered. "I mean, I had a part-time job at the front desk of an English hagwon when I was a student."

"That's just a part-time gig, so it's not the same as a real job," Gyowon countered. "A long time ago, when my mom told people she worked at K Apparel, people thought she was a designer and were impressed. She couldn't bring herself to tell them that she was a salesclerk. Growing up, I always thought, what's wrong with retail? What's wrong with having only a high school degree?"

"Nowadays things are so different. You can get clothes at chain or discount stores if they're not designer," Danhui said. "It would be more like this—a friend told me that her daughter's classmate was bragging about how her dad worked at S Group. Turned out he was an AC technician for the subcontractor's subcontractor, going all the way down like a Russian nesting doll. Anyway, the point is, there's nothing wrong with being an AC technician. His business card has the same S Group logo on it, right? I told my friend it's basically the same thing."

Yojin had only shared a few dry facts about her life, but her new neighbors were now going back and forth, assuming she was insecure about her job, taking turns digging up examples that were neither consolation nor encouragement. Yojin gave a curt nod and a wry smile. Her neighbors weren't the first to be surprised by the uncommon but increasingly less rare situation of a man staying home and his wife going to work. This had caused her to build up an inferiority complex, layer by layer, over the four years she'd been working for her cousin, a cousin she used to only see at weddings and funerals. She hadn't imagined that, even here, this would be the first question she would have to field;

then again, it would be the same wherever she went. The only difference was the degree of people's nosiness.

"Take some time to really think about it first. Once you leave the city, it's going to be hard to make it back. Look what happened to me. The building boom in my planned city is over and things are getting bad. The prices in Seoul are so high that it's impossible for me to go back, but if I could... Still, I can at least get to Seoul by subway even if I have to make a transfer or two. What are you going to do out there in the middle of nowhere?"

This had been her friend's first reaction when she heard that Yojin and her family would be moving into the Dream Future Pilot Communal Apartments.

The Dream Future Pilot Communal Apartments was a small, twelve-unit building way out in the tranquil mountains without any urban amenities, a good distance from the homes that had been halfway developed about a decade ago during a modest building boom. At first glance, it appeared to be a random inn built on a vacant lot, without even a creek nearby. Still, it was brand-new and had been built with care by the government; it was clean and the decently sized units had a good floor plan, and, most crucially, it was public rental housing. But the conditions of residency were strict and you had to handwrite a pledge as part of the twenty-odd documents required for your application.

The ad seeking potential residents had claimed the building was "just twenty minutes to city center," but that turned out to be the same fiction as listings touting an "incredibly transit-friendly area, three minutes to the subway," which described every apartment Yojin and Euno had encountered since they got married. In reality, they would have to drive at least thirty-five minutes to even get close to Gangnam and Songpa, and there were no public transit options. Beyond the remote location and lack of infrastructure, the handwritten pledge was the most stringent requirement, and depending on your values, one of the prompts could be considered insulting. The pledge itself had fanned social media discourse; in the end, two hundred and forty couples applied for the twelve open spots. Those who made it through the review and interview stages were entered into a lottery, which didn't give preference to low-income families, but rather took into account current residential status and family situation and employment.

At least one adult in the family would have an impressive job, even if they worked on contract, and both adults probably held higher degrees than the average person. It wouldn't be at all unusual for at least several of them to be open-minded and progressive on various social issues while still susceptible to looking down on a cashier. Even so, the neighbors' words rattled in Yojin's ears and crushed her chest, and that sensation morphed into the conviction that she might not quite fit in here. She felt like a transfer student joining a classroom after the friend groups had already formed.

Yojin glanced at Siyul, wondering if her daughter was also feeling that way. Siyul was the oldest child here, and she was silently drinking her juice as she studied the other kids. Yeosan and Gyowon's son, Ubin, was now sitting between five-year-old Jeongmok and three-year-old Jeonghyeop, Jaegang and Danhui's two sons, and they were crashing their wooden cars together.

"Ubin, I told you to finish eating before you play,"

scolded Gyowon, her irritation rising, and Yeosan whispered that she might wake Seah. In his arms, Seah was frowning, smacking her lips as she slept.

The recycling truck kicked up pieces of cardboard and dust as it drove off. Soda cans and bottle caps that had fallen off the back tumbled along the ground. Danhui's hands became sticky as she picked up the trash and put it in the sack.

After she cleaned up the recycling, she broomed the dust into a metal dustpan, dumped it into a trash bag, and headed up to the third floor. She could hear the baby's cries from the bottom of the stairs.

"Hyonae-ssi, are you there? Hyonae-ssi? Sounds like Darim's crying?"

She heard rustling as the crying settled, then the front door swung open. Exhausted, her eyes bloodshot, Jo Hyonae came outside holding Darim. She looked as desperate as a trembling drop of water clinging to the faucet. "Yes, what is it?" Hyonae's voice was hoarse.

"Were you sleeping all this time? You don't look like you got any rest!"

"What's going on so early in the morning?"

"Oh, Hyonae-ssi! You sent Sangnak-ssi down by himself the other day when we were all meeting the new family, and you haven't shown your face since. It's not early, everyone's gone off to work and it's already nine! I thought I told you the recycling truck comes at eight on Mondays."

Hyonae shifted Darim to her other arm and scratched her tousled head. "I had to pull an all-nighter again. I'm happy to take it on next time."

This woman was the complete opposite of the new tenant Euno, who had come out to see if he could help when he heard the truck. Even though his family was still unpacking and settling in, Euno had come out anyway and hovered about, asking if there was anything he could do, while Danhui and Gyowon waved him off, declining any assistance. What Danhui did want, although she refrained from asking, was for him to go pound on Hyonae's door and wake her up. All this time Danhui had nodded and smiled sympathetically when Hyonae claimed to be too worn-out from work to offer a hand; though she knew it wasn't that big of a deal, Danhui had been waiting for a chance to have a serious talk with that self-centered Hyonae to make sure her neighbor knew she couldn't walk all over her.

"Now you're making me feel like I'm in the wrong here," Danhui protested. "I'm not trying to imply that the work is hard. The workers collecting the recyclables are the ones doing the heavy lifting, and all we need to do is gather everything in one place so things don't go flying around everywhere."

"Right, that's why I'm saying I can be the one to handle it next time."

Danhui wanted to believe that Hyonae wasn't purposely shirking her duties, but irresponsibility and laziness seemed something of a second nature to Hyonae. Even if Hyonae herself didn't care, it was exhausting for the rest of them to have to deal with her.

"You know that's not the issue. Doing communal work together is what makes it meaningful. Like I said before, if someone does it on their own this week and someone else handles it on their own the next week, it gets tricky and the system falls apart. Even if we made a schedule of whose turn it is to do what, there are always going to be times when we can't follow it. That's why everyone needs to come out and do this together. We can be flexible when someone has an unavoidable conflict. But if you can't do the bare minimum, how will we be able to live together in harmony?"

This was when Darim, whose lips had been trembling during Danhui's speech, burst into tears again, and Hyonae took that opportunity to cut her neighbor off. "Well, I need to nurse her right now."

Danhui let out a sigh as she glanced over Hyonae's slender shoulders into her apartment—the rumpled baby blankets, an open bag of sliced bread, toys strewn across the floor, clothes thrown every which way. "Sure. Text me later once Darim's asleep. I'll stop by for a second and we can finish talking."

Danhui headed back downstairs, telling herself she shouldn't be irritated by Hyonae, who, as always, had merely given a curt nod to put an end to their conversation.

It wasn't a shock that Hyonae was exhausted—

Danhui herself had experienced this fatigue when her two boys were younger, and she wouldn't have been able to survive those years if the people around her hadn't been unconditionally accommodating and considerate. You could try your best but not make it out of the apartment on time. Sometimes, no matter how hard you tried to wake up, it felt truly impossible to pry a single eye open, even with a wailing child beside you. Raising children was all about dragging yourself forward. Despite all your maternal love and inner strength, you'd still find yourself marooned from time to time, and you had no choice but to continue on until your last breath.

Those feelings were normal, but she couldn't help but be annoyed. Whenever childcare obligations kept Danhui from upholding her side of the communal bargain (like the time she missed a general meeting at her boys' day care center), she would apologize in a manner appropriate to the magnitude of her act. She would personally deliver a handwritten note—*I'm sorry I missed the meeting, my son was sick again*—with a fruit basket or a cake box. Then she would bow in apology at the next opportunity and work twice as hard whenever a small task came her way. Even if the others were put out before, they would end up doing her a favor when she needed something; they might push her turn back or let her go first.

Long before they moved here, back when Jeongmok was a baby, Jaegang had been tied up with business, and the recycling had piled up for three weeks in the utility room of their tiny twenty-four-pyeong apartment. Of course it did; since the baby's arrival, they had started buying and using more and more personal hygiene products, and all of them had come packaged in plastic. Recycling days were once a week like at most apartment buildings in Seoul, and the residents were supposed to bring their recyclables out between six in the evening on Thursday and five thirty the following morning when the recycling truck arrived. But Jaegang had come home late after work the first week, then returned drunk off his feet from a work dinner the following week, and then had gone overseas for business the third week.

She had opened the door to the utility room to discover Styrofoam dishes and plastic recyclables piled around the large overflowing polypropylene tote bag in which they carried recycling downstairs; the plastic refuse blocked the path to the washing machine, barring her from entry. If someone were to see the utility room, they would assume she was a hoarder, the kind you saw on the news, or an alcoholic who neglected her child, and she was made miserable by this thought; it felt as though everything she had done earlier in her marriage to live a more environmentally friendly life, which of course had taken attention and effort, had gone down the drain.

Deciding to handle this problem herself instead of waiting for Jaegang to get home, she carefully slipped sleeping Jeongmok in his baby carrier. She should have done this from the get-go, but she had been trying not to expose Jeongmok to the freezing winter wind, which they'd confront on the seven-minute walk down the long corridor to the elevator and out the front doors to the trash and recycling area. Danhui went out with the bag filled with cardboard boxes and plastic. As she made the second trip with the baby on her back—after all, she only had two hands—other residents and the security guard spotted her and rushed over to help. She gratefully accepted their kindness, though she hadn't brought Jeongmok to evoke sympathy, but rather because of all the tragedies she heard about on the news, stories of a child falling or suffocating to death during the brief moments their mom washed the dishes or ran to the supermarket just across the street. By her third trip, the security guard and the residents who had been breaking down her boxes and stacking them offered to come up to her apartment to help bring the rest down.

She had, of course, bowed in gratitude, and later, once she had her wits about her, she found out which units the kind neighbors lived in and brought gifts of tteok and fruit for them and the security guard. After that, her neighbors were naturally happy to help out. This was just one of the many ways a young mother could pay back the inevitable debt she racked up among her neighbors; you just had to show your gratitude.

But Hyonae didn't bother doing any of that. It wasn't that she was incapable; she just didn't care. As an example, a salesperson hawking red ginseng or health supplements might offer a regular customer a bottle of vitamins for free, and, if that customer had any sense, they would kindly refuse after the first time, appreciating the thought behind the gesture. But Hyonae never even gave out copies of the picture books she illustrated. She claimed to be embarrassed because they weren't published by a well-known company, and said they were sold as a box set and it was therefore hard for her to give out only the one she illustrated; still, if she handed out a few books to the neighbors, whose children were all around the same age, she could easily generate some goodwill by showing everyone what kind of work she did and help them understand why she couldn't fully participate in their day-to-day schedule, but she didn't put in any effort. Relationships were like joints that creaked without fluid between them, and Danhui's biggest complaint was that the same people always felt the resulting pain and discomfort. She wasn't annoyed by the fact that she wasn't on the receiving end of niceties; she sincerely believed that these small acts were the bare minimum when you lived in an apartment building.

Even if you weren't a people person, all you had to do was merely say the right things at the right time. Reflecting on her experience raising two kids, Danhui felt that a mother had to constantly say "sorry" and "thank you" even if she had done nothing wrong. All Hyonae had to do was add just one more sentence; just now, after saying, "I had to pull an all-nighter again," she could have easily added, *I'm so sorry*. Again, it wasn't that Danhui wanted Hyonae to prostrate herself, it was just that these were the skills—or rather, the basic courtesy—of maintaining relationships. Intellectually she knew she should forgive Hyonae's disorganized disposition and not judge her based on her line of work, but her lack of social skills was obvious, sitting as she did in her room, working on projects alone.

Two days ago, Sangnak had emphasized that Hyonae had fallen asleep after meeting a deadline, which was why she couldn't come to the welcome party for the new family. He had even brought Darim to the backyard on his own to allow Hyonae to rest. But here she was, up all night again despite her husband's support. Was she drawing all the pictures in the world all by herself? Danhui had gone upstairs merely to tell her that they should try to work more effectively together, and Hyonae had cut her off, saying she'd just handle the recycling by herself the next time. Not only was it incredibly unclear when exactly this next time would be, but this disorganized approach would also render a turn-taking system useless and confusing. Maybe someone might think Hyonae was being ostracized over the trivial issue of recycling...

But it wasn't trivial.

Trivial things weren't so trivial when they piled up, not a corn on the sole of a foot or dust heaped on a forgotten shelf. Danhui just wanted Hyonae to understand this.

Hyonae was rushing to sketch a line when the tip of her 2B pencil snapped and hurtled toward Darim's face, halting the formation of the child's chubby cheek on the A4 sheet of paper. Hyonae shrieked, fearing it was headed straight into Darim's eye, but thankfully it bounced off the baby's hand clutching the bottle. Darim sat there, gnawing on the nipple, and rubbed her cheek with the back of her hand. The room was filled with other dangers—colored pencil shavings and eraser bits and small pieces of colorful paper—but Hyonae felt compelled to fling only the graphite into the trash. She was supposed to send the sketches to the agency for review today, but meeting that deadline was looking increasingly unlikely.

Now that Darim was seventeen months old, she needed to be weaned off formula and fully switched to solids, but Hyonae didn't have the energy. Hyonae could work only if Darim didn't scream and cry, and she found herself handing over the bottle whenever Darim asked for it. Hyonae seated the toddler in front of her to show her that Mom was there, and from time to time she'd glance up to make eye contact. Right now, they were sitting on the floor across a long, low table, and on Darim's baby-chair tray was an untouched bowl of broccoli and beef juk, a starchy skin cooling over it. Not that Darim had drunk a lot of formula, either. Darim met her mother's eyes and giggled and clapped, tossing aside her half-empty bottle, which sprayed drool and formula on the unfinished drawing as it thwacked Hyonae on the forehead before rolling on the floor.

Hyonae snatched a few tissues out of the box and quickly dabbed her drawing dry. Of course a child wasn't happy just because her mom existed before her eyes. You had to constantly play with her. You had to smile and cry and scrunch up your face and sing. Even as Hyonae sat there with her art supplies spread around the table, she had to keep entertaining Darim. The only other thing she managed was glancing at her phone, mindlessly tapping on headlines that caught her eye. Darim reached out, squirming and straining against the straps of her baby chair. She was about to burst into tears, and Hyonae had to move that bowl of juk before it tipped over. She wouldn't be able to send in the sketches before Sangnak came home from work. She would have to promise to submit them first thing tomorrow morning; she was destined to stay up all night again.

Not long after Darim was born, while they were still at the postpartum care center, Hyonae had to return to her work. She had completed all outstanding projects before giving birth and planned to take some time off, but life didn't always unfold the way you planned it; a book delayed by the publishing house the previous year had suddenly gone into production, and they had requested quick revisions to the illustrations. Hyonae hadn't planned on working in earnest during this time, so she began making revisions with a basic brush and paint set she'd asked Sangnak to bring over. The scent of paint filled her room and leaked into the hallway, and the nurses asked her to stop, telling her it wasn't good for newborns to breathe in the fumes. Hyonae couldn't bring herself to check out early when she had paid up front, so she pumped a huge quantity of breast milk to send into the nursery, gathered her art supplies and her pump, and dragged her limp body, as wrung out as a bunch of grapes in a juicer, to her studio. After two days of this, the nurses grew irritated, telling her it was difficult to maintain a clean environment when she kept coming and going whenever she wanted, bringing in outside germs. Hyonae ended up checking out after nine days once she was refunded about a third of her payment.

She was only in her midthirties, and hadn't expected to develop serious carpal tunnel after giving birth as the elders cautioned, but the consequences of her decision to work burrowed undetected into her body until she realized one day that pain had fully taken root.

Switching to a mouse and tablet wouldn't alleviate the pain in her destroyed wrist, but it would prove a good strategic move; for one, she could save on the cost of materials. But the change wasn't as easy as it sounded. In an ideal world, she would ease her way into the new medium, making room for plenty of trial and error as she grew accustomed to it. In the process, her style and lines might be impacted, which could cost her new work. As it was, Hyonae was already taking longer to finish projects and to book the new ones because of the baby, making it challenging for her to even attempt the switch.

All along, she had been scanning her drawings and using both a top-of-the-line computer and a professional-level tablet. But that didn't mean she was ready to move entirely over to digital illustration. With the development of incredible digital tools, it was now possible to render work in various mediums, as well as to adjust the line weight when sketching and change the precise pattern and texture of the paper, which made it hard for most people to differentiate digital illustrations from something painted on paper, but it would take Hyonae twice as long to get to the level of younger artists who were used to working that way.

On top of that, even those dabbling in art could in fact differentiate between digital and hand-drawn, and while some claimed to prefer digital illustration for its ease of corrections and intricate layers of color variation, others, including Hyonae, still preferred a hand-drawn approach. If she had to come up with an analogy, it would be like recording a string quartet using MIDI. Even with a high-performance MIDI that produced tones similar to the violin's, it wasn't comparable to a performance by musicians bowing real strings. Because of Hyonae's belief that raw materials were sacred and irreplicable—a myth that was conventional and at the same time imperious—she insisted on illustrating by hand even as she worked through wrenching pain that contorted half her body, even as she nursed or rocked a feverish Darim to sleep, and she wondered if her insistence formed some part of her hardwired drive for fulfillment and recognition.

When she began questioning her commitment to drawing by hand, it wasn't because of her physical limitations or the quickly changing landscape of illustration overall, but because of what happened with Darim.

It was around the time Darim had started crawling, before they'd moved into the Dream Future Pilot Communal Apartments. Hyonae was feeling a little more relaxed, awash with excitement and relief that they had been selected to live in the Dream Future Pilot Communal Apartments, admission for which had been very competitive despite its remote location and lack of public transportation. Hyonae drifted off after pumping, her head resting against the corner of the sofa, just as Darim decided to stick a tube of paint in her mouth. Paint leaked out of the slightly torn tube, and by the time Hyonae jolted awake, Darim's mouth and hands were dyed blue. Hyonae screamed, grabbed the baby, and ran out. Upon seeing a terrified, screaming woman holding a baby in her arms, a passerby helped her into their hired car without asking any questions.

At the emergency room, they washed out Darim's mouth and ordered various scans and took samples of blood, and concluded that since Hyonae hadn't forced her to vomit when she discovered what had happened and some time had passed by now, the paint must have reached Darim's digestive system. The doctor thought Darim must not have swallowed too much since she didn't have a rash or inflammation or any other symptoms, and suggested that Hyonae keep an eye on her over the next day.

"Kids come here after ingesting all kinds of things. It's an emergency when they swallow a coin or dice, or when something goes down the wrong pipe, or if it's something hazardous, like bleach. But it's not a big deal if they eat a little bit of sand or dust or tissues. You just have to monitor whether it comes out the other end. Once, we had a kid who drank baby bottle detergent that the mom had stored in a water bottle. That kid turned out to be fine. So, Mom, when you saw her mouth dyed blue, you probably panicked, thinking it was serious, but she likely just got a little paint around her mouth. Or it might have gotten in her mouth and she spat it out. If something was really wrong, she would be throwing up or having diarrhea or getting a rash, but she's not showing any of those symptoms, and her blood tests are normal. Earlier, when she was crying, she could have been scared because you were screaming and crying. You have to stay calm as the adult. For now, why don't we finish giving her this bag of saline, and then you can take her home. It's better to flush everything out just in case there's anything in her system."

Hyonae's taut nerves snapped like a slingshot, causing her to sink to the floor. Now that the immediate crisis was over, she wanted to get back to designing her picture-book world of trees and birds while Darim slept, hooked up to the IV. But first she was forced to tend to the blinking reality of her cell phone. She had more than twenty missed calls from Sangnak, who had come home to their empty apartment, a dozen from her in-laws and parents, alternating as though they were in competition, and one from the publishing company. Sangnak had surely rung both sets of grandparents to see if Hyonae and Darim were with them.

Once Hyonae collected herself and explained to

Sangnak what had happened, he let both sets of grandparents know that everything was okay. But he couldn't sugarcoat the truth about where she had gone with the baby; both worried grandmothers ignored the fact that Darim was fine and rushed over to Mapo from Yongin and Gimpo, respectively.

Having arrived first, Sangnak's mother suggested in a roundabout way that Hyonae was to blame, asking, "Is illustrating that children's book something you absolutely have to do right now?" Her mother-in-law's entire life revolved around her husband, a diligent, conscientious man who had spent his career as a salaried government employee; in her mother-in-law's mind, a freelancer was someone "who works whenever they feel like it." She could not understand how her son and his wife were always struggling to scrape by. Though Hyonae managed to correct her mother-in-law's misunderstanding of their financial circumstances, her misconception around freelance work was impossible to untangle, as was her belief that landing a steady, salaried job was as simple as it had been decades earlier.

Hyonae's mom arrived soon after, and when she spotted Sangnak's mother, she immediately blew up at Hyonae and swatted her on the back. "I knew this would happen when you started drawing those stupid pictures that bring in no money. As a mother, how could you not watch what your baby is putting in her mouth? How could you fall asleep with the baby right in front of you? How is that even possible? How in the world are you going to take care of her with that mindset once you move to the country? I told you to move closer to us from the beginning!"

Now Sangnak's mother, embarrassed and uncomfortable, tried to calm Hyonae's mom while failing to conceal her concerns over their move to such a remote location, saying, "Oh, we would have loved it if they moved closer to us, but the real estate prices are through the roof everywhere, in Yongin and in Gimpo, too. Anywhere would be better than Mapo, smack in the middle of the city, but they can't afford any of that, which is why they're moving there, and even though we'd love to help them stay in Seoul, our daughter's wedding is coming up and unfortunately things are tight for us. But it should be all right out there since the government built it, don't you think?"

Hyonae managed not to explode thanks to Sangnak, who ushered both grandmothers out on the grounds that an ER nurse had come up to tell him that too many people were crowding around the bed and disturbing the other patients.

Even after that incident, Hyonae kept telling herself, *Just this book*, and, *Starting with the next book*, as she put off overhauling the way she worked. According to the few colleagues she was still in touch with after having Darim, it was hard to make the switch from hand-drawn to digital, especially for picture books, which often required a variety of materials and techniques that couldn't be done by computer, like collage, engraving, and sculpture, to represent rich colors and many textures. Their experience confirmed for Hyonae that she wasn't in fact untalented or lazy, and she let out a small sigh of relief.

The one thing that had improved after marriage and childbirth was not having to listen to her friends telling her, *At least you're doing what you love*, or *You're so free*, all while she was frantic about not being paid on time and pulling all-nighters fueled by Hot6 and Red Bull. Everything else had taken a turn for the worse. Her friends with kids had showered her with gifts and congratulated her with a triumphant glee: she was just like them now. But soon enough they had fallen out of touch, too, equally buffeted by childcare. As time passed, Hyonae came to realize that when she was in the company of single people or couples without children, she behaved just how her friends had with her—announcing the results of her own unfortunate choices in a victimized air, as if the innocent person sitting across from her was the cause of her suffering—and intentionally began keeping her distance from them. To soothe her restlessness and feelings of shame that Darim was all she had left, she doggedly accepted most of the commissions coming her way, and anytime she had a few minutes to herself in the bathroom, she had the futile thought that her life had been materially better when she had to listen to her friends commenting on her supposed freedom, clueless as to what she was really dealing with.

She was sick and tired of the way publishers didn't send payments until the sixth or seventh reminder, as if they had all colluded on it. By now, Hyonae had grown accustomed to producing illustrations at high volume, many of them fueled by what remained of her youthful sensibilities after years of disappointments. She didn't expect that moving to a new place would change the rhythms of her life. A home was merely a physical space until something was achieved there; she didn't want to attach meaning to it and found it embarrassing when others did. Ninety percent of why she had applied to the housing lottery was the skyrocketing cost of rent that made it increasingly difficult to live in central Seoul. Sangnak's commute would be at least thirty minutes longer, but the new place would help chip away at the exhaustion that had accumulated over the years as they moved from one crumbling apartment to another, and allow them to enjoy a change of pace. Without an opportunity like this, they would never get to experience living in a new construction in the Gyeonggi area. And this one was provided by the government, at the lowest price per pyeong anywhere.

They hadn't had high expectations since scores of other couples had applied, but they were chosen in the end. The sheer volume of documents they had to gather was daunting, especially since they'd approached the process on a whim: they were required to submit information about their total assets, including subscription deposits, various documents for property and income taxes, records and status of payments into the national pension and insurance, along with detailed information about their line of work and medical information for the whole family. Among all those documents, the handwritten pledge was the icing on the cake—you were asked to promise to do your best to have at least three children, given that the purpose of these pilot communal apartments was to reverse the plummeting birth rate. Only those below the age of forty-two who already had at least one child were eligible to apply—in other words, heterosexual couples who had proved their ability to reproduce. Preference was given to couples with at least two children, in particular those with only one parent working outside the home. The goals of this apartment complex were clear in prioritizing reproduction, in contrast to other social welfare programs, which gave the greatest preference to grandparents raising grandchildren, followed by single parents, and only then dual-income families.

But human bodies being what they are, nobody knew whether anyone would be able to follow this mandate; couples could apply to be reimbursed for the cost of in vitro fertilization if that became necessary, and if they were unable to have three children (pregnancies included) within ten years of residence despite various efforts, they could simply move out.

They wouldn't need to pay anything back—neither for the benefits they'd reaped by having a reasonable lease nor for any normal wear and tear in the apartment. All they'd need to do was submit a doctor's note confirming that they had faithfully sought medical assistance and tried their best to fulfill their end of the contract. Without such proof, their failure to bear three children would be considered an intentional breach of contract and they would have to reimburse the government for their use of the apartment according to the terms of the agreement. When Hyonae learned that they had won a spot, this was the part that had made her feel dread. Would she really be able to have…three?

But in online moms' groups, the general opinion seemed to be that this clause wasn't a big deal.

So be it if it doesn't work out.

How could they possibly force you to go through with it?

When I think about my current problems, having to potentially reimburse the government in the future doesn't seem like the biggest issue.

And so on. Reading these opinions made her feel

a little better as she tried to imagine an unimaginable future, especially with most posters taking the carefree stance that promises weren't meant to be kept. It was really no different from missing a deadline or making a delayed loan payment. Perhaps only Kant, who had never gone anywhere without a pocket watch, kept promises and appointments like clockwork. This was a pilot program, the government must have expected all manner of trial and error, and, in fact, the program could be run into the ground or put on the back burner when a new administration took power. The other moms posted:

Why not save up while they figure it out, and then move out if things don't work out?

It's not like you're living there rent-free, so nobody will criticize you for dining and dashing, so to speak.

While the government enthusiastically pushed the Dream Future Pilot Communal Apartments, claiming the project would expand into other regions if the pilot succeeded, they all knew about the government's long history of launching various regional projects, festivals, and programs designed to inject vitality into the nation's economy, only to fritter away funds. It was easier than she thought it would be to quiet her nerves. All she had to do was close her eyes—in fact, it might even be simpler than that.

When Hyonae and her family moved in, she greeted the two couples who had already moved in during the first quarter: Sin Jaegang and Hong Danhui, and Go Yeosan and Gang Gyowon. The two families had spent a few months getting to know one another and had already formed a friendship. Hyonae felt uneasy and shy as Danhui and Gyowon welcomed them with big smiles. She couldn't shake the thought that she was as separate from them as oil paint on a watercolor canvas. This expectation became reality from day one. Danhui, surprised that Hyonae only had one child, said mildly, "Two kids are a given here, but I guess there are situations like yours, too! Good for you!" and, a little later, when she learned that Hyonae was a freelance illustrator, she exclaimed, "How lucky you are! They give preference to single-income families here. You should have bought yourself a lottery ticket with that kind of luck!"

Hyonae knew full well that her income wasn't

meaningful enough to count, and that what she did wasn't really considered work since she wasn't eligible for national health insurance; because of this, her line of work hadn't caused any problems with their paperwork. She was also familiar with the government's inconsistencies regarding single- and dual-income families, having heard about a nightmare scenario from a former coworker. She did similar work to Hyonae while her husband taught at a high school, and when they submitted documents to get on the wait list at the local government-run day care, her colleague was told that only dual-income families were eligible to apply. To prove that they were indeed dual income, that colleague brought over her income tax documents and receipts for the payments she made separately from her husband for health insurance and the national pension, but the day care had stood its ground, saying it didn't matter if she made ten won or ten million, since only proof of employment issued by a company would pass muster. In the end, her colleague had to ask a favor from one of the publishing houses with which she'd worked for a document with a vague description designating her as "employed at this company as an external planning committee member," which she was able to submit as proof of employment.

Hyonae's situation was different in that she didn't need to proactively prove she wasn't working. She had no plans to enter politics and have everything about her revealed to the world, so this kind of minor irregularity wasn't an issue for her, and in all honesty, her staying quiet about her work wouldn't meet the definition of an irregularity, since the program merely preferred, but didn't require, applicants to be single-income families. In short, there was no doubt that they met the basic eligibility requirements. But since her new neighbors, who had already moved in with unimpeachable credentials, might be annoyed by the thought that Hyonae's family had received special treatment, she vowed from that very first day to keep their interactions to the bare minimum so as not to provide them with anything to criticize.

Every day after their first encounter had unfolded like today. Danhui was the kind of person who wanted to share in every little detail of her neighbors' lives to fill a hunger for relationships that emerged from their geographic isolation. And while Hyonae didn't mean to purposely ignore Danhui and her directives, it was true that she tended to care less about working together or meeting up or handling the trash as a group. When they lived by Hongik University, she and the other neighbors, who had also been priced out of yearlong leases, hadn't made much contact with one another; here at the pilot communal apartments, though it was about the same size as her old building, the word *communal* seemed to get special emphasis. She didn't know where the *pilot* part came in, not that she had the energy to really care.

When the fourth family moved in, Hyonae figured she wouldn't need to show up to the small welcome party, and she found herself hoping that Danhui would redirect her focus on the new family. She was drained, body and mind, having completed her work in an intense spurt at the expense of several nights' sleep. She often felt that there must be a place somewhere in this world without baby bottles, and the ground beef and rice of baby food, and voices insisting on the nobility of making a home, and meetings to discuss plastic recyclables and the communal good, and by the time she put the finishing touches on a project, no matter how shoddily, she felt she could sprawl across any surface and fall fast asleep.

As she drifted off, she heard her husband telling her that the new family also had only one child, and this news brought some relief. Though perhaps she felt less relief than a yearning desire to find someone—anyone—on her wavelength.

"Whup." Jaegang got in the passenger seat with a cheery grunt. "Thanks for the ride."

The way he opened the back door and hesitated before coming up front made Yojin realize that Jaegang was as uncomfortable as she was. She figured he was grappling with how to come across as normal. She wiped the uneasy expression off her face and started the car without responding.

Upon hearing that Jaegang's SUV had gone into the shop after a fender bender, Yojin's husband, Euno, had been the one to suggest, "Why don't you drive in to work with my jipsaram?" Hearing Euno refer to her as the person at home, the common moniker for *wife*,

Yojin had almost blurted out, *Are you serious? Who are you calling jipsaram when I'm the one who goes to work?* But that actually wasn't important right now. She knew Euno had volunteered her because nobody else could carpool with Jaegang, given the logistics involved.

The pharmacy Yojin worked at was five bus stops away from Jaegang's office in the heart of the city. Sangnak left at a different time and had to get all the way to the northern tip of Seoul, while Yeosan drove in the opposite direction to his job in Gyeonggi Province. Considering the medical building's hours, Yojin had plenty of time to drop Jaegang off in front of his office before heading to work. She would just have to leave home ten minutes earlier than usual. There was no reason Yojin couldn't leave earlier as a favor for a neighbor in a tight spot, assuming, of course, that Euno could handle taking care of Siyul for those extra ten minutes. But Euno had asked her just today where Siyul's socks were, where her snacks were, where her toothpaste was; it was clear that he still relied on her to handle the details of Siyul's daily care.

Besides, Yojin should have gotten to decide whether to drop their neighbor off or not. But Euno had made the invitation as if he were her spokesperson, as if he made all the decisions for her. At that point it would have been embarrassing for Yojin to rescind the offer, even if Euno failed to clear it with her beforehand. Before Yojin could figure out whether to shake or nod her head, Danhui jumped in and tied up the matter neatly. "Oh, Yojin-ssi, that would be great. What a huge help! Yeobo, make sure you fill up their tank, okay?"

If she'd appeared visibly taken aback, they would've considered her uncooperative and unkind. Knowing she had no other choice, Yojin said, "Oh, of course, no, no need for that, I just filled the tank two nights ago." Maybe she wouldn't have felt so reluctant if she'd been the one to offer Jaegang the ride. But the mere thought made her feel like a clump of oversensitive nerves; here she was, obsessing over whether her kindness was being acknowledged, when objectively none of it really mattered.

Yojin wasn't Jaegang's personal driver, so Jaegang would have found it awkward to sit diagonally behind her, in what people referred to as the CEO's seat, but he also must have felt uncomfortable sitting next to someone else's wife. He'd quickly mulled over his choices and made the wise decision to move up to the front passenger seat; otherwise it would have seemed like he was purposely avoiding sitting beside her. Sitting side by side wasn't all that awkward anyway. It was a common occurrence in life, no different from sitting in the passenger seat of a female colleague's car on the way to a company picnic or business trip. Yojin understood Jaegang's dilemma and stayed mum, not wanting to appear irritable, but she had to admit there was something bizarre about heading to work together, sent off by more than half of their neighbors. And they'd have to be in the car together for at least forty minutes. *What in the world could we talk about to fill the strained silence?* she thought. *How long have I even known this guy? If we worked together we'd at least be able to talk about work or complain about our boss.* Perhaps thinking the same thing, Jaegang gazed out the window quietly for over ten minutes despite there being nothing to look at. Yojin wasn't the type to be sociable in every kind of situation, but it felt even more awkward when Jaegang didn't attempt any conversation, especially since he and Danhui had presented themselves as leaders of their communal apartment building. Why did she have to drive to work like this? She felt as though a part of her inner world had been invaded.

"Music?" Yojin attempted to change the mood by turning on the radio. "What do you like?"

Jaegang stayed quiet for a moment, as if unsure that she was speaking to him. "Oh, please put on whatever you like. I'm happy with anything."

"Then I'll just turn on the traffic station."

"Sure."

A nineties pop song was playing, rather than a live traffic report. Yojin considered turning it up a level or two, but not wanting to appear like she was intentionally cutting off any exchange with Jaegang, she lowered the volume and kept the music in the background. The more she thought about it, the more she couldn't believe she was spending her commute, the only time she had to herself all day, trying to be considerate and maintain a polite conversation, all for a stranger.

"Have you all settled in by now?" Jaegang seemed to be making his own attempt at conversation, so Yojin gave a big nod.

"Yes, well, it's nice that it's brand-new. It's also about two pyeong bigger than our old place. The air feels different, too, somehow." This felt safe enough, but then she wondered if Jaegang was asking not just about the apartment but also about her first impression of the other neighbors.

"And how's Siyul doing? I know kids sometimes have sensitivities in a newly built place. Like breathing issues and skin irritation."

"We didn't move in right when it was built, so I'm sure any chemicals must have aired out by now. Everything seems to be fine." Here, Yojin figured she should show some interest in him or ask about his experience. "And your… Did the kids have a hard time getting used to things when you moved in?" Yojin referred to them vaguely, unable to immediately recall their names despite having met them just a few days earlier. Jaegang had remembered Siyul's somewhat difficult to pronounce name; even though remembering one name wasn't the same as remembering two, his attention to detail on this matter made her aware of the difference in their personalities.

"A little, for the younger one. But the bigger one was fine, since he's older."

Yojin thought they would stay silent at this point, but Jaegang went on, suddenly as lively as he was when they first met. "Speaking of kids, I'm sure it won't be easy for you to send Siyul to a day care or kindergarten somewhere far. There isn't much close to us. Danhui and I have been discussing this with Yeosan-ssi's family, about how we should come up with a plan to get all the kids to play together while the parents take turns watching them. That has to be better than having them play on their own with their own boring toys, right? We're surrounded by all this nature, so we can dig a garden and sing songs and do story time and make crafts and feed them all together. Of course the important thing would be feeding them good, clean food."

"Oh...that does sound nice. Instead of leaving them to their own devices."

"We figured we should take advantage of the great outdoors, since we all made the decision to move closer to nature. Once the plan comes together, would you want to join us and chip in for the costs?"

Yojin had heard that a spot in a play-based cooperative day care with access to nature went for five million won just for the deposit on top of an additional four to five hundred thousand a month; she had no reason to decline if a reasonable amount was collected from each family and they all shared the tasks to work around one another's needs. "Well, we don't really have any set plans, and I haven't had a chance to think about that since my husband is handling that part..." She found herself hedging, sounding defensive.

"And of course we'll make a note of everything and make sure everyone can review the budget, with full transparency. Danhui is a real stickler about that kind of thing. She majored in early childhood education and worked at a day care, so she's experienced in all kinds of different activities. I swear I'm not just saying this because she's my wife, but she does have a lot of little talents, like playing the piano and making art and cooking."

Sensing traces of laughter in Jaegang's words, Yojin laughed, too. "Those aren't little talents, she's a professional! I don't have any skills like Danhui-ssi. I'm not good with my hands, and even though I took piano lessons as a kid, all I came away with was how to play a scale. And she can make art, too? That's so impressive."

"We do have an actual artist among us, but Hyonae-ssi majored in painting, and Danhui does things like arts and crafts. I don't know if you need more than that when all you're doing is teaching kids fine motor skills, but you know how they say jack-of-all-trades, master of none? That's Danhui. Anyway, we were going to see if the kids could play together and learn a little, too, since they're all around the same age. It's not to make a profit or anything like that, of course. As soon as there's some kind of specific plan, we'll share it with you and ask for your thoughts."

A day care hadn't been one of the budgetary priorities in the Dream Future Pilot Communal Apartments project. There was a home day care in the village a ten-minute drive away and a private nursery school in town twenty minutes away, but both were intended for residents of those areas; it would be hard to get quality care even if they managed to squeeze themselves in. There was a folk saying about having to button everything properly from the very beginning—because you never knew what trials and tribulations could arise from that first misbuttoned hole. In short, if everything went well, if the population grew and demand increased proportionately, a new day care would open. Until then, the residents of the new apartment building were trailblazers, a test group. Perhaps the government's choice to build an apartment complex here was to encourage the new families to gradually get to know the residents in the area, work together, and create a new communal childcare solution.

To Yojin, Jaegang's idea sounded vague and unformed. Without someone taking the lead and bringing innovation to the problem, it would be nearly impossible to launch a co-op day care program of the sort he was describing. By the time they came up with a detailed plan, cobbled together a budget, and put it in motion, Siyul might be ready to enroll in elementary school. Then Yojin would enter the grueling phase of life in which she would drive Siyul to school, send her to a nearby hagwon or after-school program, pay for daily snacks on top of the tuition, and pick her up on the way home from work. Otherwise they would need to stretch their budget and get a used car so Euno could pick her up. Whatever ended up happening, this communal day care would no longer apply to Siyul.

"Then I take it that you're on board once we figure it all out?" Jaegang asked, as though he believed things would unfold easily, as though everything was already settled.

Yojin nodded half-heartedly. "Yes. If there's anything I— If there's anything we can do, just let us know."

Now that they'd begun discussing the kids, Yojin finally felt she could survive this interminable drive. As always, kids were the best topic of conversation when making small talk with other parents. It was sometimes the only thing that parents from different economic statuses, with different societal interests and cultural preferences, had in common. Only after the birth of a child did parents experience the irony of their universe expanding while their finances shrank. Only then did they realize how deluded they'd been before kids, thinking they were financially comfortable, and that realization gave rise to an emotional insecurity, driving some to show off or obsessively compare themselves to others. Kids were often the only pure, honest link among parents, the main interest they shared.

Yojin pulled up in front of Jaegang's office. "What time should I pick you up after work? The pharmacy closes at eight—I hope that's not too late for you." By this time, Yojin's discomfort about the situation and disappointment in Euno had subsided, thanks in part to their continuing conversation; since she would have to carpool with him for a few days, she wanted to keep things friendly and make the commute pleasant.

"They only care about when we get to the office, not when we leave. You certainly don't need to come all the way back here. If I'm done sooner than eight, I'll just work a little more and then take the bus to you. We can head home from the pharmacy. And I'll cover the gas for the way back."

"Oh, no, it's really all right. You don't need to. It's only a few days."

"Please. I managed to get the platinum card today. I have to use it, otherwise I'll get an earful from Danhui." Smiling, Jaegang got out of the car as he waved a silver card, which caught the light and flashed.

"Then please let me know when you're done."

"Oh, no, I don't want you to feel rushed if I'm done sooner. Why don't you text me when you lock up? It doesn't matter what time it is. Don't worry about how I'll fill the time at the office. There's always more work to be done."

He was straightforward and matter-of-fact, refusing to give her any opportunity to object. The kind of person who everyone would consider a good man and a good employee.

The three couples had known one another for less than eight months, with Yojin's family having moved in just a week earlier; eight units still stood empty, waiting for the new families who hadn't yet finished out their current leases. Once all twelve units were filled, it would be bustling. It would finally feel like people were living here, with children's laughter and cries echoing through the building. The group agreed that they should establish a framework, lay the foundation for living communally and taking care of the kids together, since they were the ones who'd moved in first. The meeting was held at Jaegang and Danhui's, though Hyonae and Gyowon weren't present. Sangnak informed them that Darim had just thrown up and Hyonae would clean her up and get her down before coming over. And Gyowon had taken little feverish Seah to the clinic in town.

"Kids never get sick when it's convenient for the parents, do they?" commented Yeosan, Gyowon's husband.

"No, you always have to run to the ER in the middle of the night or on a weekend," said Sangnak, who added that Darim might have to be taken to the clinic as well if she vomited again in the next thirty minutes.

"Still, it's better to just have this meeting today," Jaegang said with a chuckle. "If we wait until all the kids and parents are in a good place, we won't meet until the year's out. If you could fill your wives in about what they missed, that would be great. For quick reference, I'll print out the agenda for everyone. Shall we keep going?"

"Yes, let's move on to the next point."

Jaegang and Danhui led the discussion, their ideas barreling onward purposefully like a bus entering a designated lane; even though this gathering was smaller than regular neighborhood meetings—about the size of a rotating credit association get-together at a corner store—the rest of the group seemed distracted. In college, group projects would get derailed by the slightest unrelated remark. Back then, Yojin was always anxious about making it on time to her gig tutoring a middle school student. At least she didn't need to feel so nervous about random chitchat anymore, unlike in those days. In fact, any talk of vomit or fevers was relevant, since the meeting revolved around the kids. And wasn't that the primary drive of childhood, to develop and grow and eat and sleep and soil yourself and occasionally vomit?

But the sound of the kids playing in the other room was a distraction, and it constantly screeched their conversation to a halt. The kids were living, moving, talking beings, calling for their moms every time someone hit or tripped someone else, every time they cried or laughed, every time they were thirsty or sweaty. But just because a child called out *Eomma!* didn't always mean they needed their moms; sometimes that word came tumbling out subconsciously, as if by instinct, like a reflex or a heartbeat.

Strangely, not a single child called for their dad. The kid who had fallen and gashed open their knees, the kid terrified of a cockroach—every single one of them shouted *Eomma-ya!* when in crisis, never calling for their dads or brothers or sisters. Yojin remembered the time when she was ten and living alone with her grandfather. She'd almost stepped on a dead rat in their yard and screamed *Eomma!* without quite realizing what was coming out of her mouth, which brought her grandfather running over to slap her on the back with his bony hand instead of soothing her. Because she was calling for her mother, who'd left her and failed to keep in touch. Yojin had no idea how she was supposed to stop that reflexive reaction, or how she was supposed to remember she didn't have a mom and should change course midscream to yell out *Appa!* or *Harabeoji!* instead. As she grew up, Yojin would wonder why people universally cried out *Eomma!* when they were scared or startled, eventually coming to the conclusion that *eomma* was a modified version of the exclamation *eomeona!* or *oh, my!* But the etymology wasn't entirely clear, and it could have been that *eomeona* had derived from *eomma*. When she learned about Carl Jung in her college cultural psychology class, she wondered if the word *eomma* was just one example of the collective unconscious that was said to be genetically encoded. What if all of humanity could make the concerted effort to dismantle the collective unconscious from this point forward, starting at home, consistently guiding kids to ask for their dads and not their moms if something happened, much like her grandfather had with her, and slowly manipulate that gene for the future? Then maybe the use of the word *eomma* would only remain on everyone's tongues like a vestigial organ...

Crash. With the sound of shattering glass, Yojin's

aimless, floating thoughts scattered. Before she could determine what had happened, her body sprang up and a scream ripped out of her throat. "No, don't touch it!"

She dashed over to Siyul, who was about to pick up a shard of glass. Yojin paused. All the kids were looking up at her, frightened. She'd become the type of person who detected a nice breeze and blared a tornado siren.

"I'll clean it up," she mumbled by way of explanation. "Only grown-ups should touch glass."

Only when Siyul stepped back into safety did Yojin notice that Ubin's hand was bleeding. "Did you get hurt? Are you okay? Can you show me?"

But Ubin's lip trembled before he burst into tears. He didn't seem to be crying out of pain or because of his bloody hand.

"Oh, boy. Are we going to end up taking both kids to the clinic today?" Yeosan came over and picked up his son by the armpits. "Let's take a look."

Danhui brought over a plastic bag and a damp paper towel. "Here, just put the big pieces in. Be careful. I'll wipe up the little pieces and the dust with this. Yojin-ssi, I can do it."

"No, let me help."

"It's easier and neater for one person to do it. We don't need everyone getting hurt. Hey, kids, go stand behind Yojin Ajumma. Don't step over here. Careful, careful—there you go. Of course I should clean it, Yojin-ssi, it's our apartment and our cup. I thought I put it all away, but I didn't see this one here. My fault."

"It's not a big deal, just a graze," Yeosan reported. "There's no glass in his hand. I'll just wash it off." He placidly carried Ubin into the bathroom and turned on the faucet.

"Just a graze?" Yojin asked. "But he's crying so hard."

Yeosan laughed. "I don't think he's crying because he's hurt. He got scared when you yelled, Yojin-ssi. He probably thought he did something wrong. It's all good now. It's no problem at all."

Yojin flushed. Everyone else was calm; she was the only one to overreact, bringing the meeting to a halt.

Siyul, for her part, raised her voice to be heard over Ubin's sobs. "I told him not to touch it. But then he did and it fell."

"Okay, okay," Yojin responded absently, not wanting to focus solely on her child in front of all her neighbors.

Jaegang smiled and shook his head. "I'll summarize what we discussed so far and hand it out. You can check the boxes for what you'd like and get it back to me, and I'd be happy to pull it all together."

"I'm sorry to make more work for you," Yojin said. "I shouldn't have overreacted."

"Oh, no, not at all! We can never have a full conversation when the kids are around anyway. Their safety is the biggest priority. Anyone else would have done the same thing."

Anyone else... But Yojin was the only person who'd bounded out of her seat and screamed. She sensed that Jaegang had noticed her mortification and was attempting to make her feel better. Maybe Yeosan and Jaegang and Danhui were more relaxed because they had two kids and were more accustomed to the chaos. Since Darim wasn't there, Sangnak could be forgiven for not paying close attention to the kids, but shouldn't Euno have done something? If he had any paternal instincts, wouldn't he have reacted, even if it waylaid their meeting? Realizing how useless her earlier stray thoughts had been, Yojin gave a bitter smile.

But for Jaegang and Danhui to enthusiastically lead the charge and act like elected representatives just because they were the first family to move in…

Yojin had always felt socially awkward and only kept in touch with two friends. In school, she'd only taken on minor responsibilities, like collecting notebooks for her row or taking her turn as group leader. Danhui, on the other hand, had eagerly informed her about everything from the moment they met and tried to insert herself into all kinds of matters, and Yojin wondered if she should consider this characteristic a positive one. Maybe Danhui and Jaegang were just friendly, not nosy, and being helpful came naturally to them. Was Yojin like them, ready to melt into anything like cane sugar? Could she be the type of person who moved through the world lightly and rhythmically, bending like a dancer's limbs without getting pushed off course? And if she couldn't, how would she navigate her current reality?

The next day, Yojin went down the checklist she received from Jaegang and circled which activities she wanted Siyul to participate in. Gardening. Music appreciation and singing. Various crafts, including origami. Art making. Physical activities, including dance and percussion. Seasonal traditional games. Reading and storytelling. If all of these activities could be implemented, even if a bit clumsily, they would have a program as good as any highly rated day care. After all, they were merely a group of ordinary parents—with one early childhood education veteran. She didn't expect this co-op to be systematic or professional. It would be more than enough for the kids to play together and pass the time under adult supervision.

The main point of this was to fill the days. A child's work was to pass the time in any way possible while steadily growing the number of cells in their body. An adult's work was to watch that child and mostly to suffer through that time, to let it pass by, then turn a new page. You'd encourage the child to draw an odd new shape. To color it an unexpected hue. All while your own existence grew fuzzier by the day, until you were reduced to a sketch of yourself, and, in the end, you were rubbed out by an eraser.

Really, Euno was the best person to be tasked with hauling things in the middle of a weekday. Danhui and Euno drove Danhui and Jaegang's car to the big-box store in town while Hyonae and Gyowon watched the rest of the kids. This new development dashed Yojin's assumption that carpooling with Jaegang would come to an end when his car was fixed, and she found herself getting used to commuting with her neighbor.

The day before, Yojin had wondered out loud whether it wouldn't be less of a hassle to order school supplies and different types of craft paper and food online, but Danhui had said it was best to check out the items in person first, note the product and brand, and buy online next time. Danhui had insisted that they go to an all-natural organic grocery store, and Yojin had backed down, figuring that Danhui, with her experience, would know better. After all, this was for the kids. Yojin felt ashamed that she'd been tossing Siyul cheap toys leaching endocrine disrupters, completely unaware that they were harmful. In the month she'd gotten to know her, it seemed to Yojin that Danhui had created a perfectly balanced, elegant life for herself and her family. She'd also come to understand how easily Danhui could intimidate others. Whenever she observed Danhui in action, Yojin felt criminally imperfect, even though she'd never once had the desire to intimately understand the word *perfection*.

Danhui tapped on KakaoTalk at a red light and found Gyowon's message, accompanied by a crying emoji. It was an SOS. Hyonae-ssi wasn't being very helpful and was having a hard time even watching her own child. Siyul, in fact, was being more helpful, looking after the little kids like she was the grown-up. Please don't take too long picking things out and come back as soon as you can.

Euno caught the tense smile flitting across Danhui's face. "Something wrong?"

The light turned green and Danhui shrugged as she eased her foot off the brakes. "No, it's just—this happened often when I worked in childcare. Not every parent is collaborative."

"Oh, I see." Euno's nod conveyed minimal sympathy. He didn't entirely understand the conflicts that could arise between a childcare provider and a parent, more specifically a female caregiver and a mom, interactions that generally happened between women; these were aspects of life he wouldn't have even known existed had he not had Siyul.

"Gyowon-ssi is asking us to come back ASAP. She's saying Hyonae-ssi is having a hard time controlling the kids, that it's too much. I mean, we're just getting to the store!"

"I see."

"Is that it?"

"I'm sorry?"

Danhui's tone sharpened into the same one she took when nitpicking her younger husband, Jaegang. "Gyowon-ssi says Siyul is more helpful than Hyonae-ssi, who's the adult."

"Is she?"

"Are you only going to understand if I spell it out for you? That your daughter is going to be doing all the work until we get back?"

She was an expert at explaining every little detail, building up to a climax, tightening her grip on her conversation partner's nerves. This was how, for example, she had navigated a situation in the past: *I went all the way to the postpartum center with both kids to see your brother's wife. I had one on my back and one by the hand, and I couldn't go in because kids aren't allowed. I had to ask them to deliver our gift and then I had to come all the way back home. Didn't I tell you that I looked it up online and kids aren't allowed? And that nobody's allowed in these days except for the husband? But you said you had to go to a work dinner. You didn't listen to what I was telling you. You said there's no way they wouldn't let family enter. Now do you understand what I was saying? After I went all the way there for no reason? Didn't I tell you that you should listen to me? Didn't I? So now what do you think you should do for my sister, who had* her *baby three months ago already? You didn't even call them when she had the baby, saying you were so busy with your project or whatever. But then did you ever do anything? What do you think you should do at this point? Let me hear you say it with your own mouth.* Shuddering at Danhui's tone of voice, Jaegang had made some time that weekend to go visit her sister and family on his own.

"Oh, sure, I get it," Euno said. "But Siyul's a good girl and she watches her cousins, too. I'm sure everything will be fine."

"And you think that's okay?"

"Are we playing Twenty Questions? You can tell me directly if you think something should be done." Euno wasn't so dense as to not notice Danhui's sudden irritation, but he couldn't understand what caused it. Everything had seemed fine when they left. Gyowon's message had just arrived. To him, it didn't seem like a big deal that Gyowon was asking them to come back quickly when things were getting hard back home.

"No, that's fine." Danhui knew that trying to get Euno to understand the essence of the issue in the few minutes it would take them to get to the store would be like expecting him to decipher the lyrics to a Latin hymn he was hearing for the first time. If such a thing were possible, she wouldn't have had so many fights with Jaegang over the years.

"To be honest, I don't really know what to do when

women react this way. Yojin does this sometimes, too. She's always saying, 'Do I need to spell it out for you, can't you just think of it on your own?' But of course it has to be spelled out. That's why we have language, isn't it? And men's and women's cognitive systems are very different. You can't ignore evolutionary psychology—it's been studied for decades. When I say that, Yojin's always like, 'You're blaming structures and evolution and whatever because you don't want to think about it. You make me do all the mental labor that goes into thinking about things and weighing the pros and cons, and you just want to do what someone else tells you to do.'"

Once, Jaegang had made similar excuses to Danhui, citing as evidence an experiment he saw in a foreign documentary film. Researchers had stuck electrodes or chips or something all over a man's and a woman's heads and had them watch TV. The man was able to focus on the show and not notice someone trying to get his attention, but the woman was distracted by her kids calling for her and the phone and doorbell ringing, her attention splintering toward the gas range or a steaming iron. From the outside it appeared that she was multitasking, but in reality she wasn't able to focus on any one thing. Although over a decade had passed since he'd seen that documentary, he claimed that its conclusion justified the fundamental differences between men's and women's brain structures and ability to focus.

"I'm in agreement with Yojin-ssi there," Danhui said.

"Then this is how I would respond. Don't think of a man as a human being. Think of him as an animal that understands what to do only when you order him to do it, every single time. Point with your finger because we're really good at doing what we're told. If we get a clear input, we deliver a clear output. Even I think that a man is like a child or a dog."

What did a child or a dog do to deserve to be recruited into these excuses? "I'm not interested in whether men think they are children or dogs. Are you saying you're proud of being like a child or a dog?"

"It has nothing to do with being proud of it. It's just— How do I say this? It's just that this has already been established, so there's nothing anyone can do about it. Life doesn't follow logic or reason, does it? The people who are able to think more flexibly and expansively should be generous and take the initiative to set the example and say, *You do this, I'll do that.*

So that life can go on smoothly. Life can't be quantified and divided. You can't approach it by saying, *I'm thinking about this one issue this much, so you have to think about it exactly this much, too.*"

"It must be convenient to live like that." Danhui's voice climbed an octave, as though to shake off her thoughts on the topic. "Let's forget about it. I was just a little annoyed. I'll just focus on driving."

Even if she pointed, would he look at what the finger was pointing at or would he look at the finger? Danhui shook her head in exasperation, but Euno's words were as real as muscles that tensed when flexed. They revealed a specific, even useful, option, that you'd be forced to take barring a foolproof alternative. In truth, whenever the caregivers had to leave the apartment complex, their roles were automatically delineated without anyone needing to make suggestions or adjustments. Euno carried the heavy things; that was more effective than leaving the physically strongest person with the kids and having only women go to the store. And most people would understand instinctively what kind of unmanageable scene would unfold if a man were assigned to watch all those kids alone.

It was only now that they were living in communal housing that Jaegang volunteered for various tasks. But before they moved here, if she ever asked him to watch the kids, he would literally just look at them. One weekend, Danhui and her sister-in-law had gone food shopping for Jaegang's mother's birthday, and she had left the kids with him. As it was too close to dinner by the time they finished shopping, they grabbed something to eat at the food court, and when she returned home, she found Jaegang dozing on the couch with his arms crossed—at least he was demonstrating a modicum of duty and conscientiousness by not fully stretching out and snoring—as the boys wrestled, mopping the floor with their bodies, amid ripped and crumpled sketchbooks and broken crayon nubs and spilled water and sticky traces of juice trickling out of plastic cups flung on their sides next to take-out bowls of jjajangmyeon and snack bags leaking crumbs. Most of the clean laundry, which she had folded and placed in a basket next to the TV, had been tossed around and stained by pieces of jjajang-covered onions and remnants of various snacks, and the boys had trampled all across the linoleum floor, smashing crayons to bits.

She could have taken the generous route and considered it inevitable for their home to be in a constant state of chaos by virtue of having two young boys, and she was all too familiar with how unmanageable the living room could get despite constant cleaning and tidying, but the biggest issue was that both boys were three days into a cold and they had to take medication twice a day, after lunch and dinner; their meds were still in the paper envelope they came in. As she ran the jjajang-smeared laundry, she asked Jaegang if he understood what it meant to watch the kids, and his response had been just like Euno's. *If you don't write down instructions and put it on the fridge with information on how much medicine to pour into which cup and what time to give it, how would I know what to do? They have to take different medications and they have different dosages. Who knows what might happen if I give them the wrong thing? If you don't explain it to me clearly and patiently, how would I know what to do?*

When Danhui flipped out, Jaegang treated her as though *she* were being unreasonable; he told her that a cold lasted a week with medicine and seven days without, then even threw a counterpunch at the end: *Remember what my parents said to you when our parents met for the first time? They said, we hope you'll fix him up and make him useful. I know they were smiling when they said that, but you know they weren't joking.*

And that was what she had done this whole time. She had fixed him up and made him useful. He wasn't quite up to her standards yet, but Jaegang did grow up a lot over the last couple of years. Danhui expertly backed the car into a parking spot and gritted her teeth, not entirely knowing what she was bracing herself for.

Yojin flinched at the knock on her window. She unlocked the doors and Jaegang got in the passenger seat, careful not to jostle the big paper bag he had in his arms.

"I'm sorry you had to wait. I know I said I was going to be done soon."

"That's okay. It was easy to find parking and I had a book to read, so I wasn't bored."

One time became two times, and once something happens twice, it has the tendency to become a habit, Yojin knew. While Jaegang's car was in the shop, he would avoid working late and meet her at the pharmacy when they lowered the shutters at eight. But once they had a rhythm going, Yojin realized how intensely Jaegang worked to avoid staying late, and at some point she started going to his office and waiting for him there. Jaegang validated parking for her in the lot beneath the office tower. It was fairly bright for an underground parking garage and she stayed inside with the engine off and the doors locked, but it was still somewhat creepy to be in a garage after most people had gone home. She could have gone to a nearby café, but she didn't think the cost of a drink was worth the short amount of time she had to wait.

Last time, she had waited about twenty or thirty minutes, but today she'd had to wait slightly over an hour. It still wasn't that bad considering how late an average office worker stayed. Jaegang seemed to prefer not to go out for dinner but to grab something quick in the office, or finish all his work and pick something up on the way home. That was how she knew that the bag Jaegang brought contained snacks from his office.

"You could have stayed later and had dinner with your colleagues," Yojin said. "Our kids will already be asleep when we get home either way."

"But you haven't had dinner yet, either, right?"

The pharmacy closed at an odd time, so she would either have an early dinner with her cousin or grab a late snack; like many office workers, she lived with a constant stomachache and bloating because of her inconsistent mealtimes. The pharmacy carried all kinds of medicine, including those that would help her stomach issues, but Yojin was sick of even looking at the boxes lining the shelves.

Jaegang opened the paper bag. "That's why I brought you some. My coworkers brought them in. They're individually wrapped. Nobody's even touched them. I don't know if you'd like any of these, but please help yourself if you're hungry."

The baked goods were packaged with buzzwords like *whole-grain*, *rye*, *gluten-free*, *butter-free*, *sugar-free*, *milk-free*, and so on. While they all looked healthy, Yojin had the feeling she wouldn't really like how they tasted.

"Thank you."

She took the smallest bread in acknowledgment of his thoughtful gesture—and also because she was indeed feeling peckish—and turned on the engine.

Jaegang placed a hand lightly on the wheel. "Why don't we head back after you're done? I know you like to keep both hands on the wheel. Or I'm happy to drive if that's all right with you."

"Oh, no, that's okay."

The car wasn't new or nice, but Yojin still felt a vague resistance at the thought of entrusting someone else to drive it. She took a huge bite, making her cheeks bulge, and Jaegang laughed.

"Take your time."

Two of his fingers brushed her face as though they were lightly pinching her cheek or maybe brushing off some crumbs, and Yojin froze. She didn't know what to do with the bread in her hand; she was so shocked that she wasn't sure if she should just drop it on the floor, but of course none of this was the poor bread's fault.

"Aren't you going to have some?" Yojin asked the question in an attempt to pretend he hadn't touched her like that.

"I had some earlier while I was working. Go ahead, you can have it all. You're enjoying it so much, it's cute."

A raisin caught in her throat. The rough texture of the whole wheat—or was it rye?—bread sandpapered the top of her mouth and scraped her throat as it went down. She didn't want to appear flustered, so she just looked straight ahead and shoved the rest in her mouth. She mumbled, "Put your seat belt on. Let's go."

None of it meant anything. She repeated that to herself as if casting a spell, trying to convince herself that she wasn't the sensitive type who assigned intention to every single unthinking gesture. She stepped on the gas, feeling on the side of her face Jaegang's smiling gaze, which she told herself was innocent. Yojin wasn't a twenty-year-old college student; she had survived too much to ruminate on an inadvertent touch or gaze. She'd worked so many part-time and temp jobs from a young age and had been touched inappropriately at all of them; that sort of behavior was standard on film sets where, as an extra, she had to wait around for hours in the cold and the rain and the wind (that she had met Euno during that time was something else), and after marriage, she had valiantly lain on a university hospital bed as trainee obstetricians in white coats came and went and prodded her below the waist, rarely telling her, *I'll be checking to see how far the baby has dropped, this might be a little uncomfortable*, before conducting their exam. She was now a thirty-six-year-old woman who had become numb to it all.

Only when she held Siyul in her arms for the first time did Yojin understand what her friends with kids had kept telling her: *You only become an adult once you have a baby. Before that, it's just playing house.* At first, Yojin had thought her friends were trying to convince themselves as much as her. A reassuring gesture, uttered through gritted teeth. A way to make themselves feel productive, despite the fact that having children had derailed their lives and shunted their individuality and desires to the periphery. What she hadn't realized was that these words actually functioned as self-defense. Becoming an adult meant you became shameless, or, if you weren't fully shameless, you became someone who covered that sense of shame with a shoddy lid or stitched it closed with fraying nylon thread. Any woman climbing onto the exam table at the ob-gyn's office was forced to recognize that her body no longer reacted to any stimulation or insult; it was now an inanimate object, incapable of annoyance or sorrow. Those who followed what was often considered the normal route were inured to most physical contact. A relaxing numbness draped over you once you resigned yourself to not react—if you considered yourself an object, you couldn't get exhausted. As she nursed Siyul, a thought tore through her that maybe ajummas—the universal embodiment of toughness and violence and shamelessness, middle-aged women who cut in line and shoved their way through a crowd and threw their bags across the aisle to claim a seat on public transit and elbowed their way loudly to the front to get a few extra samples at the store—had become that way after enduring an onslaught of inappropriate looks and touches.

That was why Yojin wasn't planning to confront Jaegang about what happened, even though he had clearly touched her face, whether on purpose or by accident. She tried to convince herself that all men's fingers were like flies settling for a moment wherever they wanted, rubbing their legs together before flying away; it was her fault for not having managed to swing the flyswatter in time.

Without even taking her socks off, Yojin sprawled her exhausted body across the bed and looked at Siyul, who had apparently fallen asleep moments ago. She spotted a small scratch below her daughter's eye in the dim glow of the night-light. Did she forget to clip Siyul's nails after her bath two days ago?

Euno noticed where her gaze had landed. "Ubin did that with a toy car." He explained that Ubin had been swinging the car around, making vrooming and whooshing sounds, and the side mirror had scraped Siyul's face.

"So a car accident, then," Yojin joked wryly, guessing that, as a man, Euno would have had a hard time intervening over an accidental injury that happened while the kids were playing.

"Before I could say anything, Gyowon-ssi sat both of them down and told Ubin, 'Tell Nuna you're sorry and that you won't do that ever again.' And then to Siyul, 'Let's forgive him, since he's apologized.' I mean, it's not great for a girl to have a scar on her face, but—"

"What else is there to do other than forgive him? Kids get cuts easily, but I'm sure it'll fade just as quickly."

Even if Euno hadn't come out like that, Yojin had been planning to react with generosity. As always, whether or not an incident needed to be escalated into an argument among grown-ups hinged on the size and the depth of the cut. If it had been a knife rather than a toy that had injured Siyul, Yojin would never accept an apology, even if the perpetrator's mom yanked her kid over and said, *You better beg for forgiveness!* She would insist on a sincere gesture of regret in the form of monetary compensation as a way to demand accountability from the mom who didn't watch her child close enough, though she was well aware that most incidents involving kids tended to be outside anyone's control.

Now, if it hadn't been a scratch, if a bone had been broken, she would obviously rely on available legal remedies, but then Yojin realized that she didn't know what you were supposed to do about invisible injuries or internal wounds that didn't have objective criteria to check off. It occurred to her that the scratchiness in her throat that she had attributed to a raisin or a kernel of rye was the beginnings of a cold. Should she ask Siyul in the morning how she'd felt when she was clocked by the toy car, or would it have the opposite effect of reminding Siyul of something she'd already forgotten...? As she worried over what to do, her tired eyelids blinked, then closed fully.

The key point is that we've collectively decided to raise the kids communally, focusing on their growth and emotional state. This is not a situation where we get the kids together, then go off to do our own thing. Let's not think about it as a chance to take a break by having all the kids in one place. Even if it takes a little more effort, we have to share the burden together. Do we all agree on this point?

Danhui had emphasized this part during that initial meeting. Nothing good came from being stuck at home, dealing with the kids by yourself while your spouse was at work, feeling lost and depressed that you were alone in the trenches. You might even end up letting the kids fend for themselves. To combat this, they would care for all the kids together as a trial run, sharing and communicating deliberately, for the long-term health of both the children and the parents. Even if nothing meaningful resulted from this experiment, at least the kids would play together in the same space; it was reasonable to assume that this arrangement would do no harm, especially when the alternative for the kids was watching videos or playing games on smartphones like little zombies. Even though they were mostly too young to have developed enough fine motor skills to do much of anything, it was still better for them to play with one another.

Each family brought out toys made of wood or soft cloth, along with age-appropriate teaching aids and blocks. The items were sprayed with a natural disinfectant and dried in the sun for an entire day. They distributed groceries purchased out of the pooled budget so that each family could make a few banchan and soup in bulk according to the menu plan; they would bring them over to Danhui's when it was their turn, and Danhui would steam the pesticide-free rice daily.

Once the plan was set, Yojin woke up an hour early on days she was scheduled to cook and made rolled omelets and braised beef in soy sauce and sautéed small anchovies or seaweed. She had to leave early for work, so she prepared basic banchan. Meanwhile, Gyowon, an excellent cook, made a different soup nearly every time and whipped up impressive dishes like daikon radish wraps and maekjeok. It would have been logical for Euno to take on the cooking instead of Yojin, but like many men, Euno had never made a thing until Yojin began working at the pharmacy; he'd never cooked before they got married, not even after Siyul was born.

It wouldn't be fair to pin Euno's lack of skills entirely on his and his parents' indifference. He had led an irregular life to go all in on his art, his days and nights swapped, moving from one monthly rental to another with his roommates. The staple for anyone cash-strapped and adrift was instant ramen, which he could make by pouring hot water in the cup it came in; he would boil ramen in a pot when he wanted to show off. Yojin believed the act of cooking revealed someone's relative emotional breathing space, and as she struggled with Euno's inability to cook, she often thought about the bachelors depicted in the Japanese novels she'd read as a student. Regardless of its relevance to the plot, those men were always hand-making pasta, plating it, and decanting Chilean wine of such and such vintage, but she knew the truth of the matter, even without having to recall those elegant but solitary fictional dining tables. She had been in charge of housework from a young age, asking her grandfather for money when she needed it, so she knew from experience how the act of washing and tearing and chopping and boiling required time and money, and, most importantly, a healthy, capacious mind and body.

With Siyul's birth, it became pointless for their small family to buy groceries only to let them wilt and get tossed, unused, so she'd stopped cooking, especially since Euno was often away from home for long periods to attend film-related meetings without much to show for it. She got used to buying even the smallest handful of kongnamul muchim instead of making it herself. She didn't labor over homemade beef broth and pureed carrots as first-time moms tended to do, instead feeding Siyul Gerber purees from the store or ordering precooked baby food, and this habit became even more entrenched when Yojin began working at the pharmacy and Euno decided to stay home, discouraged as he was by his repeated failures and disappointments, his ideas and synopses and treatments and even a draft screenplay taken by others without any recognition.

So it had been years since Yojin had hauled out cooking implements and bustled around the kitchen. As she anxiously made the first batch of banchan for the kids, she failed to season them properly and burned some of the ingredients. But she could only imagine if Euno were to be entrusted with the cooking; it would negatively impact all the families. She thought it ironic that she was making food from scratch for Siyul now, when she hadn't even done this for her as a baby.

But her physical exhaustion and the feeling of being towed along by a cause she hadn't signed up for melted away like snow at the beginning of a thaw when Siyul talked about how much she liked that day's songs and dances, how good the food was, how Appa had acted out the story as he read them a picture book, and how she had a good time except for when Jeongmok kept interrupting and Jeonghyeop ran around being loud. With Yojin going to work, Euno, who didn't have expertise in anything save movies—it wasn't like he could teach young children about film formats or mise-en-scènes—would have to be tasked with story time, leading physical activities that didn't require a sense of rhythm, and outdoor play. If she considered what was on his plate, making a huge amount of banchan once a week was an easy lift, as long as the others didn't take issue over the amount of sugar or soy sauce she used or questioned whether the oil was organic and the salt was sourced from within Korea.

The second time Yojin delivered her banchan, Danhui popped by with an armful of sauces and seasonings she'd apparently purchased from some co-op. Yojin was dumbfounded. She managed to smile when Danhui told her, *We shouldn't use regular oil to stir-fry the good anchovies we managed to buy for the kids. They're not the cheap kind you can get at any old supermarket. I hope you don't mind, since this is for everyone.* Once Danhui left, Yojin dropped the bundle on the table and glanced at the mirror by the shoe cabinet. *My smile was natural, not pinched, right? I looked like I was truly grateful to Danhui, who's mindful of every single little detail, and didn't show my annoyance, right?*

Six kids and three adults ventured out for the morning walk. Hyonae pushed Seah's stroller, Euno pushed Darim's, and Danhui corralled the four remaining kids, who were walking hand in hand down the sidewalk.

"Ubin," she commanded, "don't go off to the side, walk down the middle. Jeonghyeop, hold Nuna's hand tight, okay?"

Gyowon would be preparing lunch while the group headed to the valley creek and back.

On their walk Hyonae looked distracted. Darim kept poking her head out of the stroller and calling, "Eomma! Eomma!" but Hyonae just flashed a smile and didn't respond. Her head was swimming with the deadline she'd missed and the half-finished watercolor drying out on her desk. She couldn't sketch or paint anything as she watched her skills and desires, inseparable as they were from the daily grind, yellow and harden like forgotten two-day-old rice.

Everything had been decided by Sangnak while Hyonae was asleep or frazzled by Darim being sick. When she finally learned what had been put into motion, Hyonae had fought with her husband, hissing as quietly as she could, "Are you insane? Why would you agree to all that and check all those boxes on your own? I'm the one at home. You go to work all day and don't have to worry about any of this. I'm the one who has to do it all. Does it look like I have all this free time on my hands?"

Sangnak had frowned and shrugged, not all that invested in the idea, either. "It wasn't like I rushed to sign up. But there's only four families, so it would've looked bad if we didn't join in when everyone else was agreeing. We have to get along with other people and learn how to live in a community. Think about it. You're always talking about how you never get to draw during the day because you're feeding Darim and cleaning up after her and washing her. If you can't meet your deadlines anyway, isn't it better to tire her out by having her play with the other kids so she gets to bed earlier, instead of struggling to keep her entertained? Then wouldn't you have more time to work at night?"

Sangnak's naivete was giving Hyonae a splitting headache. "You really think it's that easy? You think it makes sense for a bunch of us to watch a bunch of kids during the day and get even more exhausted instead of just watching one kid? What do you think I am..." *Made of steel?* she almost added, the words hanging at the end of her vocal cords before falling away. If she said that, Sangnak would no doubt suggest she quit freelancing if she couldn't make this work—an unhelpful solution. Hyonae was aware that she was taking things out on Sangnak; she knew that even if she had been present at that meeting, she wouldn't have been able to blurt out, *Oh, we're not interested*, when everyone else was on board. She knew the repercussions of dissenting, and while she herself didn't care about all the whispers that would follow, she at least wanted to spare Darim. She truly hadn't anticipated having to worry about these issues when she decided to join a communal apartment complex. Forge friendships? Get close with one another? Raise the kids together? Share inane smiles and conversations, as though closeness were something that could be snapped into place like Lego blocks?

Once the co-op day care began, though, Darim left home each morning excited about the new routine, and she certainly looked happier than when she used to play on her own. Intellectually, Hyonae knew that, as a parent, she should be grateful. When she looked back on how hard she'd worked to cobble together a career, she knew she wasn't in a place right now to make satisfactory illustrations. But it would be great if Darim could at least grow up happy and healthy. For that to happen, Hyonae herself had to be like a dog or a bird in the corner of a dynamic group portrait, an ignored animal unable to draw anyone's gaze.

For about ten days, she felt buoyed by this change in perspective and the feeling of satisfaction. But then, as she frantically came up with daily activities, leading kids who obviously couldn't follow directions, producing crayon-drawn pictures and making salt paintings and molding sculptures with clay and paper blocks, she found that she didn't feel ownership over a single thing. To make things worse, Darim was too young to participate in arts and crafts; the younger kids were on the other side of the room with Gyowon and Euno, who entertained them and played music for them, dealing with their daily plight of dirty diapers and empty bottles of formula. It became clear that the babies and preschoolers were merely sharing the same physical space rather than spending time together. By the third week, Hyonae couldn't help but feel like she was losing out somehow. Wouldn't it have been better to watch Darim on her own, even if it was hard? Wouldn't it have made more sense to spend her days turning on the radio for classical music, playing with toys, and then, when Darim finally went down for a languid nap, rushing to color a blank page even if it was in fits and starts, even if she had to keep stopping in the middle, even if she never had time to draw in the pupils of her character's eyes?

The kids were put down for a nap together like at a regular day care, and Hyonae's regrets accumulated every nap time. She couldn't tell the others that she would head home to work while the kids were sleeping. Even if they were made to lie down, each child drifted off at a different time, playing with the edge of their blanket, and six-year-old Siyul, who really was much too old to nap, would flop around on her mat, her eyes wide-open, not understanding why she had to rest, and even once most of the kids were finally asleep, Danhui would either sit down and begin filling out the activity log or head into the kitchen with an *Oof, why don't we take a break ourselves? I'll make some tea. What would you like?* For Hyonae, the most dissonant part of this was the realization that Danhui wasn't doing this for some underhanded reason, but as an extension of a natural, everyday gesture. Danhui was the kind of person who would automatically come to this conclusion: *Since people are in my home and the kids are asleep, now is the time for us to sit around with tea and chat.* Without paying any mind as to whether they all wanted to get to know one another.

Gyowon would stretch and pull her chair up to the table as though she'd been waiting for Danhui's invitation, and Euno, who had held back at first, wondering if he could join the women, no longer hesitated, approaching Danhui easily and offering to help make some tea. The treats Danhui brought out to accompany their tea tended to be baked goods like warm madeleines, which would summon Proust's first sentence before even touching anyone's lips. They'd probably have looked like aristocrats in a Western painting, leisurely enjoying an elegant tea, if it wasn't for the fact that they were taking a short break during nap time. It was a beautiful, perfectly balanced composition, a scene familiar to Hyonae; she knew how to pin down its essence in a painting.

But were they close enough to spend forty minutes of precious free time staring at one another? She didn't think she could get away with it each time, but every three days or so she would stand up, smile, and tell them she had to urgently wrap something up. "Can you message me when they're awake? I'll come right down."

After about a month of this, she began to feel burned out, like the vast majority of working moms constantly juggling their careers and housework and childcare. Since the day care was in someone else's home, Hyonae felt she had to always be on, unable to rest or throw herself on the sofa. She felt like a ball being smacked around in three-cushion billiards, and if she didn't do something soon, both about this feeling and her rage toward Sangnak, who was doing a whole lot of nothing despite having signed them up for this, she would go insane.

She had to get herself out of this situation and pick up a paintbrush.

She approached Euno and murmured discreetly, "Can we swap strollers when we get to the valley?"

"Oh, sure, I don't mind either way."

"Darim has actually had a light fever since yesterday, so I don't think she should go in the water. And she might get the other kids sick. Maybe I should keep her home for a few days. We'll head back early."

"I'm sorry to hear that. Is she feeling okay? Do you want to switch now?"

"I'm sure it's nothing. I'm just being overly cautious. Kids are always sick, aren't they? Hopefully she'll be catching fewer bugs when she's Siyul's age." Hyonae kept looking straight ahead, ignoring Danhui's chilly gaze skewering the side of her face. As the wind changed direction, she caught a whiff of manure.

This wasn't all that surprising since they were surrounded by fields, but when she sniffed a little harder, she could tell it was a slightly different smell. Sure, they were similarly displeasing, but manure was imbued with a modicum of earthiness, like ash, and something organic and well fermented and fertile that conjured images of flourishing crops and golden fields. What she smelled right now was the excrement of livestock, the stench of waste that wasn't used for anything. More precisely, it reeked like a sty, the kind of all-consuming stink that couldn't be scrubbed away even when you hosed it down every day.

Of course, it wasn't unusual for a sty to be near farms, and it went without saying that excrement existed wherever animals lived. That was when Jeongmok shouted, "Ew!" and grabbed his nose, dropping Jeonghyeop's hand. Siyul frowned a little without saying anything, like an adult, but Hyonae had no way of knowing that the girl reacted that way because she had a stuffy nose and couldn't smell very well.

Have you had lunch?

Why was he texting her such a random question? Yojin placed her phone face down on the counter and handed the credit card back to a customer who had purchased something to help with digestion. Staff at medical practices generally took their lunch break about an hour after most offices, while pharmacies tended to be less consistent with their breaks. Many of the doctor's offices in the medical building took a break starting at one or one thirty to better serve nearby office workers stopping by during their lunch hour. She'd never explained the ins and outs of pharmacy work to Jaegang, so it wasn't too surprising for him to ask about lunch at only twelve forty, but she still ignored the message; they weren't close enough to check in beyond carpooling matters. They had never made sure the other person had eaten lunch or asked how the other person's day was going. Her phone buzzed twice more and her cousin shot her a look.

I'm nearby for a meeting.

Lunch if you're free?

At this point I should just send a quick reply to make sure there's no misunderstanding, she thought. Yojin took the next customer's prescription and filled it, then tapped out a response. It'll be hard to get away, we usually go after 1:30. We take turns so I'm not sure when I can take lunch. Sorry, I'll pick you up later. She hesitated a few seconds, then added a smiley face at the end. That should be good enough. Hopefully it didn't sound too terse. A few minutes later, a bear sticker holding an OK sign arrived, and she was relieved that her message had landed the way she'd intended. Maybe they should cool it with the carpooling unless their spouses needed a car, like if Danhui needed to go to the market or the kids were going to a puppet show or amusement park. She didn't necessarily think Jaegang had any ulterior motives, but there was no reason to create opportunities for awkwardness and ambiguity.

He wouldn't—he shouldn't—have any other motive. In fact, the very thought that he might have some other motive, even if the possibility was as tiny as a pepper flake stuck between teeth, was itself wrong, when all he'd done was demonstrate thoughtfulness to his neighbor. She couldn't, in all seriousness, ask him why he was texting her something like that when they weren't really that close. She could be imagining something that wasn't there and end up humiliated. It had to be that his conception of a friendly, neighborly relationship was different from hers; she was someone who thought it best not to bother neighbors unless you truly needed something.

But then, five minutes after her cousin left for lunch, Yojin, hearing the tinkle of the door chime, got up from the counter, and was stunned to see Jaegang striding in. But she couldn't question it. He'd mentioned he was nearby, and he was certainly free to stop in if he felt like it. Maybe he'd developed a sudden stomachache.

"What brings you here?" she asked.

"What choice did I have when you're playing hard to get? I had to come over, didn't I?"

Playing hard to get? What was he talking about? Yojin didn't have the presence of mind to question his choice of words. "I have to stay here until my cousin comes back."

"I see. You must have had a lot of people come through during lunch, what with all the offices around here. You'll be eating lunch really late, won't you?"

"I've been on this schedule for years, so I'm used to it now. What about you? Have you had lunch?"

"Yes, I grabbed a quick bite with my client. I figured you'd be stuck here, so I brought this for you on my way back to the office." Jaegang placed a warm paper bag on the counter.

"Oh, this is too much. When my cousin's back I'm going to go grab something, and we can't have the pharmacy smelling like food. As you can see, we don't have any windows."

Yojin didn't want to tell him that sometimes, in the summer, they left the door open, blasted the AC and the air purifier, and got delivery.

"Then you can bring this out to a sunny spot when it's time for you to take lunch. There are so many little parklets, what with all the office buildings around here. I didn't mean to make you uncomfortable. You can give it away if you don't want it."

Now she felt she was overreacting. Jaegang seemed not to care who ate the food, and it occurred to Yojin that her firm refusal might make it appear that she was making this out to be a bigger deal than it was. Plus, he wasn't planning to stay here with her; he had to get back to work himself. "Just this once, then. Thank you. I'll share it with my cousin when she gets back."

"Oh, I don't think it'll be enough to share."

"Well, anyway, next time, no matter where you take meetings, please don't bring food over."

"It's just because I feel bad that you give me a ride so often. I'm so grateful for that."

"Not at all, I have to come to work, too. And you also fill the tank for us, so I think you're actually at a loss. You shouldn't keep charging the platinum card."

"This time it was the gold."

Yojin took this to mean that Jaegang had used his own credit card, one that he didn't share with Danhui. "Well, thank you again. I'll see you after work."

Through the floor-to-ceiling glass wall, she watched Jaegang waiting to cross the street. When the light turned green, he looked back at the pharmacy and waved, smiling, and she returned the gesture, feeling that she couldn't ignore him, though she couldn't tell if he could see her from the outside. Then she opened the warm bag. It was stamped with the logo of a café famous for brunch, so she already knew it wasn't a simple snack of bungeoppang or deep-fried blood sausage; still, she was taken aback when she pulled out a pretty package containing a bacon omelet, shrimp-and-broccoli salad, and roasted potatoes topped with shredded cheese. A quick glance at the bounty informed her that it would have cost quite a lot, certainly a dizzying sum for anyone who had to work the calculator to stay on budget. It wasn't half bad to be treated so well, but this gift was too expensive for an ordinary office worker to hand a neighbor. Yojin wasn't sure how to point out its excessiveness so that he wouldn't do this again. But on a more basic level, she wondered if she was abnormal for considering this excessive in the first place, and if making an issue out of it was an inconsiderate response to another person's kindness.

While she agonized, she speared a morsel of omelet with the plastic fork that came with the food and put it in her mouth, where it melted on her tongue. Her teeth and tongue mashed the delicious fluffy egg and the perfectly cooked pieces of bell pepper and onion and carrot. Given her wallet, it was the nicest, fanciest lunch she'd had the opportunity to try. She wondered what sort of expression she should wear on her face when she went to pick him up later.

It sounded like a dining chair falling over. The noise didn't seem to be from something heavy, like a couch or a bookcase. They would have to call an ambulance if something like that had fallen over, whether by accident or because of a natural disaster. Did someone try to move something and drop it? At this hour? Why didn't they wait until morning?

Hyonae was awake anyway because of a deadline she'd pushed back nearly a month, but she was afraid that Darim, who'd always been a light sleeper, would wake up from the thud. It didn't sound like the noise had come from right above them; maybe from next door. But a building like this, with more empty units than not and people scattered throughout, was like a mouth with missing teeth; it wasn't unusual for sounds to travel and spread in all directions, standing as it did in the middle of nowhere without any nearby structures. It was no use trying to pinpoint the source. None of it mattered anyhow, as long as Darim stayed sleeping.

Under the pale light, Hyonae brought her wet brush close to the bear's face, but flinched. Now it sounded like two people grappling and falling. She heard a low scream. Did they fall while changing a light bulb? Even if she tried to put a positive spin on it, it wasn't the kind of noise you'd hear during lovemaking. Not to mention that it would be embarrassing for all involved to hear noises like that in this living environment; these were people she would see tomorrow.

It would probably depend on the couple, but who would be having sex anyway, when their bodies and minds had turned ragged from bearing and rearing children? Hyonae and Sangnak had naturally found themselves in a drought as they went on with their daily lives. Hyonae, who never got a break, day or night, wasn't able to do much for Sangnak when he came home after work, and Sangnak, for his part, was understanding. Who knew if he really understood, but at the very least he was aware of the overgrown thicket of reality that bound them with insistent thorns. While Sangnak slept, Hyonae changed Darim and soothed her and breastfed her and never managed to cobble together more than a consecutive hour of sleep for days on end, which rendered lovemaking an artifact of ancient times. Once in a blue moon, when Darim slept through the night, they would blearily attempt sex with a sense of duty and obligation, knowing that things couldn't continue like this, but soon Hyonae would shift away in pain. When she brought it up at her regular checkup, the doctor told her that it might feel more painful and sensitive because the inner wall of her vagina had thinned from childbirth and reassured her that things would gradually improve, but Hyonae was terrified every time they tried and could never follow through, which made her worried about how they would manage to have three kids.

Even putting aside individual differences, it would be hard to have sex in a place with such thin walls and so few neighbors—

"You… Aaaahh!"

An incomprehensible scream split the air as Hyonae

thought, *And I guess it would be hard to have fights, too.* Fights cropped up everywhere, as naturally as drawing a breath, but she hadn't considered the possibility of being subjected to such inconveniences by moving into a communal building in the middle of nowhere, where you quickly learned exactly how many bowls and spoons another family owned. After all, people applied for a spot to live a happy life; they didn't begin the application process by first demanding to see if the floor plans might muffle their verbal altercations. The scream that had just ripped through the night might have been an attempt to say, *You asshole*, but the screamer's own ire had eviscerated the precise words. A wife was enraged at her husband. Or maybe she was resisting as her husband pushed or hit her. Should they do something? Soon she could hear a man yelling, a threatening voice that wove between the woman's screams, with a child's cries mixed in. Which family was it? She couldn't tell from the sound of the crying child whether it was a boy or a girl, and even if the family had two kids, they might not be crying at the same time. She couldn't pinpoint who it might be. And still came the sounds of something falling and bumping, screaming, furniture clattering...

Hyonae's paintbrush was drying up. Darim started to fuss, her eyes still mercifully closed, and Sangnak sat up sleepily.

"What a racket. They really should keep it down."

"Should we call the police?"

Another crash, and the child's wails grew louder. "Stop. Stop!"

"Who'd come out for a fight between a husband and a wife?"

"It's different these days. Should I call? Do you think?" Hyonae was starting to feel anxious. She was neither the type to care about other people's issues nor all that interested in finding out who was fighting, but it was a different story if someone was getting beaten up. She wasn't so hardened that she could focus on her painting and ignore the ruckus coming from somewhere close.

"I'm sure they'll stop eventually." Now that he was awake, Sangnak got out of bed, scratching his head, and went to the bathroom.

Hyonae put her brush down and went to Darim, who was whimpering, and patted her on the chest. Regardless of who was fighting, how awkward was it going to be to face their neighbors tomorrow?

In their previous apartment, they had of course been surrounded by sounds of friction and differences in opinion. That building had felt cramped compared to their current one, the front doors mere steps apart, the units with suboptimal layouts, and the bearing walls carrying sound even more clearly than in their new place. Their neighbors were mostly unmarried couples and singles, and she would often hear them having sex. Because of this, even in the middle of the day, Hyonae would creep up the stairs as quietly as possible. But it was a different situation back then, because all kinds of people with different living arrangements and routines and schedules lived there, and the building was situated in an alley by a busy street, tightly packed with commercial buildings and apartments, which led to a flood of civil complaints about drunken fights and noise, among other issues. Even if you bumped into the people you thought were responsible for the ruckus the next day, you would go your own way without making eye contact. She wasn't nosy enough to ask neighbors a decade younger than her what happened the night before, and she especially didn't want to be seen as a meddling ajumma tired of her own life, who had no interest in anything other than rumors and gossip.

Now that people of similar ages and lifestyles were living here, isolated together in a remote location, forced to chat every day about whatever topics arose from the communal care of their children...maybe if a child didn't show up tomorrow that would be the clue that their parents were the ones fighting. Even if they didn't call the police, should they go over and attempt to pull them apart? Which was being a better neighbor, ignoring it completely or attempting to mediate and calming them down? If the arguing couple had any common sense, they would stop out of embarrassment if nothing else once the neighbors rushed over, but was it really better to get them to pack their feelings inside instead of detonating their rage, all out of consideration for others? Then again, didn't a neighbor have the right to say something? The fight was so loud in the middle of the night, disturbing everyone's sleep.

As these thoughts flitted through her head and tangled together, a blunt thud traveled clean through the shouts and wailing. If they didn't stop soon, whether it was a criminal situation or sex, it wouldn't be out of bounds for someone to go investigate the source of the noise and knock on their door, just to ask, *Can we get some sleep here?* But then again, she didn't want to be the kind of person who rushed out in excitement to consume someone else's misfortune, to gawk.

"You ass… I…and rip it all…all the time…that… I'll…" The couple's shrieks and hollers were unintelligible, pulverized, but her ears caught something about a guarantee and then something about stocks. The fight had to do with finances.

Of course it did. Couples always fought over finances. But no big conflict ever arose from one single source. Even if the words *guarantee* and *stocks* sounded serious, as long as the family's belongings weren't about to be red tagged, as long as they weren't going to be thrown out onto the streets, this topic might have branched out from something else. It could have all started when the wife discovered a mysterious expenditure on the husband's cell phone or a suggestive text from another woman. Or it could have started somewhere even less significant, like a family group chat.

Hyonae knew all about this. She'd been sick of watching the incoherent exchange of political talk and gossipy health tips that proliferated in the eight-person

KakaoTalk group chat they were in with her mother-in-law and father-in-law, Sangnak's sister and her husband, and Sangnak's brother and his wife, but she was too afraid of upsetting the family to leave the group. It wasn't until Sangnak's sister's husband said, **You have to vote for so-and-so this election**, and sent a link to an article, that she got fed up enough to exit the chat. She gave some excuse about needing to delete the app, but the move caused a falling-out with her sister-in-law. It was during the ensuing fight with Sangnak that she calculated exactly how much money they'd given to his sister for her wedding. Irate, Sangnak had shoved her by the shoulders, and though she had fallen gently, she'd gone straight to the doctor for a note indicating that her injuries would take four weeks to heal, all to teach him a lesson. When she got there, she also learned she was pregnant with Darim, and, overwhelmed by despair and her conflicted feelings over the news, she'd decided to be admitted to the hospital right then and there. Horrified that he'd shoved his pregnant wife, Sangnak had come to her eight-person room to grovel for forgiveness, causing the other patients to laugh and tell her to forgive him; that was how their fight had fizzled out.

"Shut up. Let go! I said get lost! What the...?"

Something crashed; someone must have fallen to the floor. Darim finally woke up and began crying, and Hyonae patted her on the chest to settle her. She heard several front doors opening and closing heavily in the corridor.

"Whose apartment is it?"

"What's going on? Be careful."

It was unclear who was speaking and who was being addressed; the words mixed and broke limply apart in the air.

Sangnak flushed the toilet and grabbed his windbreaker from the back of a chair. "I guess the others went out. I'll go take a look. Stay here with Darim."

It would be better for Sangnak to go if the situation required someone to physically separate the couple. Hyonae forced herself to smile at Darim, who looked around with tears in her eyes, and held her. The baby blinked slowly, unable to push off the weight of sleep hanging on her eyelids, and soon began breathing evenly. Hyonae didn't have the mental space in the moment to decide if they should move to a place where they could fight freely, especially since this wasn't a realistic option for them, but the feeling that it would be hard to live here for as long as they had been hoping, regardless of how many children they might have, prickled like a cold sore.

The next morning, despite the incident, every single child made it to Danhui's apartment. The only changes were that their day had begun about an hour later than usual, and that Gyowon, who nearly always cooked the main dishes at home and brought them over, wasn't present.

No one had sustained a serious injury the previous night, but Gyowon had bled significantly after bashing the side of her forehead against the corner of the TV stand, and Yeosan's neck and cheeks had been scratched, though he was bleeding less than his wife. When the neighbors had gathered and knocked, Yeosan had been the one to open the door. He'd calmly greeted the neighbors with a look of relief and offered his apologies about the noise; his demeanor suggested that he hadn't been the instigator, but rather that Gyowon had irrationally flipped out. The neighbors exchanged awkward glances until Jaegang dragged Yeosan out, saying they should go for a smoke. Sangnak, who knew that neither man smoked, looked helplessly from person to person and followed them out, while Gyowon let out a leonine roar and burst into tears as she collapsed on the floor.

"Excuse us," Euno and Yojin said, as they went inside and soothed the crying kids. In the living room Danhui grabbed a tissue and pressed it to Gyowon's bleeding head.

"I know, I know," Danhui said. "Try to calm down. Take a deep breath." An avalanche of wails buried Euno's concerned question about whether they should call an ambulance.

The bleeding didn't stop, though they applied pressure to the wound, so eventually Euno took Gyowon to the emergency room. Gyowon had refused to get in the car with Yeosan, and no one thought it was a good idea for Yeosan to drive in his emotional state.

Euno was caught off guard when the front desk staff and emergency room personnel repeatedly asked, like an automated message, if he was the patient's husband. "No, I'm her neighbor, just the neighbor." He felt uncomfortable as he awkwardly sat waiting by Gyowon's bed, while she slept off a sedative after getting some stitches on her forehead.

How in the world did he end up bringing someone

else's wife to the emergency room? How did he end up being the one waiting for the medical staff to finish treating his neighbor and texting her husband to keep him informed? Still, the situation being what it was, he overcame his feeling of discomfort and ended up sending the driest, most concise text ever written. *Nothing to worry about. They say scarring will be minimal.* Yeosan sent him a short message back. *Thank you.* There was nothing more, no apology to the person who'd been auctioned off to watch over his wife and wait for her to be done so he could drive her home like her chauffeur.

It was already around ten in the morning by the time he got Gyowon back home; she'd been given a bag of fluids through her IV and woken up. By that time, everyone who worked outside the home had left, including Yeosan. Euno helped Gyowon—who was so upset that Yeosan had uncaringly gone off to work without resolving their fight that she was on the verge of collapse—all the way to her apartment, though even Euno, who didn't have a job, knew that without some sort of natural disaster or serious accident, Yeosan wouldn't have been able to take the day off, certainly not for some emotional turmoil and minor scratches on his cheek.

Danhui came by with a tray holding a pot of abalone juk she had somehow already made and a kettle of barley tea and placed it on the bedside table. She told Gyowon not to worry about anything, that they would watch Seah and Ubin until dinnertime so she could rest, and then left the apartment with Euno.

"It won't be good for the kids to stay with their mom when she's not stable mentally or physically. Did Gyowon-ssi say anything on your way back? Like why they fought?"

Euno shook his head, remembering how he had stared straight ahead, hands on the wheel, without saying a word. "No, should I have asked her about it? I just let her rest in the back seat because she seemed so unwell."

Danhui scoffed and waved a hand. "No, that's not what I meant. I just thought she would have offered an excuse since they were so loud and woke everyone up, like, this was what actually happened, or something like that. Then we'd at least be able to sympathize with her. Right? I mean, everyone slept terribly because of them and had to go to work exhausted.

Isn't it frustrating to know that they fought and we don't know why?"

Euno felt a chilly distance from her words, which seemed to suggest that neighbors had every right to hear the full context of a marital argument as compensation for breaking up a fight in the middle of the night. "Well, I was only at the hospital, so... Did Jaegang-ssi give you any clue about what happened?"

They were now in front of Danhui's apartment, and could hear the kids singing from the other side of the door.

"A clue? Oh, please. He just said, 'I don't really know, I guess there must be some reason for it.' That was it." Danhui opened her front door.

Ubin was sitting at a distance from the others, quietly holding a toy as though the shock of seeing his parents' fight was still fresh in his mind, and Seah, although she was still too young to understand what had happened, must have been exhausted by the negative energy; she was asleep in the room closest to the front door.

Yojin and Jaegang drove to work while Euno remained at the emergency room with Gyowon. This was the first time Yojin was riding in Jaegang's car, and she'd made a show of stamping her feet so as not to bring dirt into the car, feeling intimidated by its well-maintained exterior, and, once inside, the roomy interior. Though she had seen the Ford Explorer parked in front of their apartment building, it felt different to be riding in it. Jaegang must have felt cramped in her ten-year-old compact by comparison.

"So what do you think happened last night?" As soon as she uttered this question, mostly to fill the silence, she realized how irresponsible it sounded. She looked like a gossip. To hedge, she murmured, "I mean, we all do that sometimes, of course."

"Yojin-ssi, have you had that big of a fight before?"

"We've shouted and thrown things, but it's usually something that doesn't break, stuff that's easy to clean up. Like a box of tissues or a plastic tray or something. We've never drawn blood, even accidentally."

"Wow, how have you been able to survive without brawling this whole time? You must be so frustrated," Jaegang joked, making an exaggerated shrug, and Yojin folded away her guilt about gossiping and laughed.

"What do you mean, frustrated? You don't fight as

a stress-reliever. You end up fighting because things aren't working out the way you want them to. You can't live like that, fighting every other day."

"That does make me wonder. Maybe it's because you're living such a quiet life, but I want to hear what you sound like when you scream."

I want to hear what you sound like when you scream? What was he going on about? Yojin hesitated at this turn of phrase, potentially suggestive depending on how you looked at it, and turned toward the window. "How about this? Next time we fight, you can come over, like we all did last night. Then you can see for yourself."

Jaegang laughed. "Don't go out of your way to pick a fight for me."

As always, Jaegang's words and actions stopped precariously close to crossing the line. And since everyone's line was drawn in different places, it wouldn't be unreasonable for Yojin to cut him off and refuse to play along. If she truly felt uncomfortable and put off, that would mean he had crossed the line, but she'd hold back until he said or did something that was obviously, universally off-color. She didn't want to make things awkward for them both by getting offended by every single thing that might be considered off-putting. She especially didn't want to be thought of as an exhausting, overly sensitive neighbor who went to the mat over a throwaway joke. She wanted to be seen as a wise, intelligent person who knew how to respond appropriately to a lighthearted joke. Even before she'd moved into this small, quiet, isolated communal apartment building, really since she'd begun ringing up countless sick people at the pharmacy, Yojin had honed her ability to be hospitable and treat everyone with respect.

More than anything else, she didn't appreciate that she was the one who had to assume a stern expression, that she even had to calibrate her reaction in the first place. Whatever happened, she didn't want to be in the ludicrous position of having to demand, *What exactly do you mean by that?* Nobody in the world would forthrightly reveal their intentions in the face of such a half-hearted protest, which meant that she would be forced to explain what she detected: *What do you mean, you want to hear someone else's wife screaming? Isn't* that *what you mean? I don't know what your intention was but you're making me uncomfortable. Even if you were joking, I'd appreciate it if you don't say things like that going forward.* Then he would tsk, appalled, and shake his head, saying, *Wow, I guess I can't say anything. How could you think what I said meant* that? In fact, it was possible that others would point at her and laugh: *If your mind instantly goes to sex when all he said was I want to hear you scream, that's on you, you're the one fixating on something X-rated.* There was something unsatisfactory in how words alone failed to capture the meaning behind Jaegang's subtle gestures, the way she took in what he said, and the way the vibe between them shifted in an instant.

It would be a relief if all that happened was that she offended him and he thought nothing more of it, but more often a moment like this became a juicy morsel of gossip and spread all over town. *Can you believe how she talked to him? What kind of lifestyle must she have, what kind of thoughts must she have, for her to interpret what he said in that way? Has anyone ever said they wanted to sleep with her, or that they wanted to watch her do it, or anything like that? She should remember what she looks like and how old she is before accusing people. She must be a little deluded...* Whether it stemmed from a misunderstanding or reality, once she was branded as the one who brought upheaval to the community, it would pulverize all her relationships with the neighbors; it would no longer be possible to live among them, in a building they'd only just moved into. Yojin gave herself a thumbs-up for not stiffening in her seat and for taking the comment for the joke it was.

"I'll come pick you up at eight." Jaegang pulled over across from the pharmacy.

Trying not to show the discomfort she felt by their roles being swapped, Yojin said, "It's no problem if you're delayed, so please don't feel like you have to rush on my behalf."

In her mind, the priority and hierarchy were clear: Jaegang was a permanent employee and the head of his household, while Yojin was doing a temp job she could quit at any point. In fact, a pharmacy assistant was a job for someone who lived near the pharmacy and could come and go easily, but she didn't feel she could quit since she was related to the pharmacist. Her cousin, too, seemed to feel bad that Yojin was coming in every day despite having moved so far away, but as she was well aware of Yojin's financial situation, she didn't suggest that she find a new job.

"Please don't worry about that," Jaegang said with a laugh. "Or is it that you want to spend that much more time with me?" He gave Yojin a pat on the back as she got out.

Of course it wasn't that they would be spending more time together, it was just that they would leave the city later... Yojin hunched her shoulders defensively and didn't look back.

When they got home, they found Euno and Danhui standing side by side in front of the building, as though waiting to greet them.

"What are you doing out here?" Yojin got out of the car first and tilted her head in confusion. Why were they standing there like coconspirators, their body language noticeably tense in the faint moonlight?

"Yeah, how would you have known when we'd be back?" Jaegang asked as he got out, but Danhui ignored him to address Yojin.

"It's so sad that you only get to see Siyul asleep by the time you get home! Does working at a pharmacy mean you always have to stay so late?"

Yojin was taken aback by Danhui's unexpected question; they were a mere twenty minutes later than usual. "It's in a very busy neighborhood, especially because we're right next to a medical building."

Of course, Yojin could have phrased it differently; she could have said, *We hit heavy traffic today*, or she could have said something closer to the truth: *We're late because of Jaegang-ssi's schedule, not mine. We might have gotten home even later but Jaegang-ssi managed to wrap things up quickly.* But Danhui's show of concern for Yojin was in truth an underhanded reprimand, the kind of nosiness she wouldn't even tolerate from her parents or in-laws. Yojin's response, emphasizing that she hadn't been out having fun somewhere in lieu of coming home, underscored her irritation.

Jaegang closed the driver's door and joined the conversation. "We're late because of me. You know that. Is everything okay?"

"Right, right. That's not important. Yojin-ssi, I wanted to tell you this in person so you wouldn't be too shocked. Earlier, Siyul—"

"What happened to Siyul?" Yojin's voice turned sharp at her daughter's name.

Euno spoke up as if to defend Danhui. "She got into a little fight. With the kids."

"A fight? With kids who are all younger than her?" Yojin stopped herself from adding, *But Siyul isn't the kind of kid who gets in fights.* She knew enough about communal living to understand that claiming her child would never do such a thing was something she could pull out only as a last resort.

"Why don't we go inside and talk?" Jaegang nudged Danhui forward and led the group in.

Yojin had been cognizant that when a six-year-old, and a girl at that, was among infants and toddlers, she would naturally be expected to look after the younger kids. But she figured that Siyul's behavior wouldn't shift drastically just from the change in environment, especially since she was an only child. Learning to get along with other kids would be beneficial for her, and Euno had thought nothing of it, either, believing that it would be a dress rehearsal of sorts for becoming an older sister. Today, Siyul had stayed right by Ubin and Seah, who weren't in a great mood, to make sure they had their pick of toys, and during art class she had pushed crayons and colored paper toward Ubin. Euno hadn't noticed her taking care of the kids, but Hyonae did.

Once Hyonae pointed out Siyul's generosity, Euno grew more attentive and found she was indeed being considerate. Euno was proud that Siyul was thoughtful and empathetic, as was to be expected for a girl, but then Jeonghyeop had come over and thwacked her on the head, jealous that she was being nice to Ubin. Taken aback, Siyul pushed him and he fell. Then, before anyone could intervene, Jeongmok had run into the fray, kicking Siyul and pulling her hair. Hyonae had been changing Seah's and Darim's diapers in the other room and Danhui had been laying out the afternoon snacks. This second attack happened while Euno was helping Jeonghyeop up, and it took him a minute to pull Jeongmok off Siyul. The ruckus made Ubin cry. By the time everything had settled, Euno presided over a chorus of four wailing kids.

Even without Gyowon, who was asleep after taking some medicine, there were still three adults present, but it was true that, in reality, the number of adults made no difference once an incident escalated. Siyul had fallen and hit her mouth on the floor, resulting in a bloody upper lip, but her teeth were intact.

At first blush, the incident sounded like something that could have happened at any day care or preschool, and Yojin understood why the adults hadn't been able to physically control the situation. Most importantly, since she wasn't present at the time, she didn't feel she had the right to make the judgment that adult negligence had led to the skirmish. She also understood that Danhui had brought the kids together and made the boys apologize for their actions.

But there was something else gnawing at Yojin's crumpled feelings. Why, when there were three adults there, was Siyul put in a position to have to look after the other kids? Even if nobody had assigned Siyul that job, how did those circumstances arise so naturally? What's more, Yojin felt alienated by Euno's report of what he had told Siyul before bed, when she must have been nursing upset feelings. *Siyul,* he'd said, *since you're a good girl and the oldest, you'll forgive them, right? Jeonghyeop likes you so much, and he was sad that you were looking after Ubin. That's why he ended up acting like that, by accident. He's young and doesn't know any better, so let's forgive him, okay?*

It was entirely possible that Yojin might have said something similar to Siyul after such an incident if their roles had been reversed. But if it were up to Yojin, she might have made sure, from the very beginning, not to put such a burden on Siyul, even if it hadn't been intentional. Whether Siyul felt that to be her duty, whether she thought it was burdensome or enjoyable, was a separate issue.

"She stopped bleeding pretty quickly, but I think there will be a little swelling when she wakes up tomorrow. I was so worried and felt so bad—I wanted to give you this." Danhui opened a drawer in the TV stand and took out a small cosmetics box. "It's a natural, handmade ointment with the gentlest of ingredients. A mom I know makes this herself. When Siyul wakes up tomorrow, make sure to put this on her lip. You can apply it as often as you want. Here, keep it. Use it for Siyul."

Yojin silently spun the package around in her hands. The words coming out of Danhui's mouth—*jojoba oil* and *dong quai* and *shea butter* and *chameleon plant* and *eucalyptus*—failed to resonate.

Euno started speaking, and Yojin came to her senses. "Now you're making us feel bad. You're being so considerate! It's fine, really. These things happen with kids."

"Thank you, Euno-ssi, that does make me feel a little better. But it's not the same with kids. Siyul might still be upset for a while. Tomorrow, Gyowon-ssi is supposed to be back, and I'll be right next to them the whole time, making sure nothing like this happens again. Does that sound good?"

Danhui was being so apologetic, but the best Yojin could do was offer a rigid smile and change the subject. "Speaking of, how's Gyowon-ssi doing?"

"She slept like the dead. But what choice does she have? She has to think about her kids! She'll have to get a grip on herself. And to top it off, Yeosan-ssi apparently had to go overnight somewhere for some workshop or other. I'm sure things will be a little frosty for a while when he gets back, but they'll manage to go on."

A little frosty and then manage to go on. Was this really what life was? They would surely bury this incident like it was a valuable piece of gold, and at the next opportunity they would dig it up to make an even bigger hole. Was that marriage? Yojin thought about the long list of things she had buried instead of continuing to argue them out with Euno. Because she didn't want to break the precarious peace they'd managed to create. She didn't want Siyul to witness their fights. They had bigger problems. The elders in their family were ill and...

She counted up the days she had pushed their problems aside without solving them, pushed them aside to render them invisible. She recalled the emotions she'd entombed deeper than remains in a grave, alongside realizations that were buried like relics, thoughts and feelings too indulgent for an ordinary life.

How could she add a second child to this? Adding a third on top of that would be entering the territory of the surreal, separate from considerations of advances in medicine, her physical strength and immune system, or the desire to form, through community building, a world that still felt livable.

This was why she couldn't tell him. Yojin couldn't tell Euno what had happened; it wasn't the kind of thing she could bring up when they were dealing with Siyul and her injury. She couldn't tell him what Jaegang had done on the ride home. To effectively describe that ambiguous situation so that Euno would understand required an unbelievably precise thought process and an incredible amount of energy.

Jaegang had told her about an article he'd read online earlier in the day, and Yojin had nodded along; she had heard about the incident as well. *Think about it*, Jaegang had said. *If you grab someone to save them, just once, and they get all upset, why would you try to help anyone out in the future? It's too fraught. Don't you agree? Like if I grab you and hold you by the waist, would you get upset?*

Say I pull you in really fast so you don't fall, but then it turns out we're too close and I touch some part of your body, like the chest or the butt, somewhere like that. Shouldn't I get a pass? Yojin had laughed awkwardly: *I'm sure it must be hard to be an emergency worker because of that. But why do you keep using me as an example?* And Jaegang had replied, *Oh, I'm just making a point.*

Yojin wasn't sure if she was allowed to be offended just because he talked about waists and chests despite never having actually touched her, and more critically, she wasn't sure Euno would sympathize or have any reaction over mere words, when he had advised his own child to forgive and be understanding despite her being injured by a kid who wasn't all that much younger. As someone who had fiddled with screenplays and treatments for so long, he understood intimately that words were meaningless until they manifested before your eyes in a tangible form, through a specific act.

The only way forward was to act as though nothing had happened. She would consider the words that had emerged from Jaegang's mouth to have evaporated into the air, having never been put into motion.

Even so, Yojin was typing *mini recorder* in the search bar of her browser, though it was unclear to her yet how she'd use it.

Everything was nice and quiet once the two brothers, the most energetic, rowdiest of the six kids, were gone. If Gyowon, who was still on edge, were to add her own exaggerated interpretation, she would say it was so quiet that she could hear the creek hundreds of meters away.

Danhui had already taken Jeongmok and Jeonghyeop to her parents' home to celebrate her father's seventieth birthday that weekend, and Jaegang was planning to come home after work and then head over there tomorrow. Hyonae had left yesterday to be with her mother-in-law, who was due to have breast cancer surgery. Hyonae's parents would watch Darim while Hyonae slept on the cot in the hospital room until her mother-in-law was ready to go home. She'd likely be gone for ten, maybe fifteen, days.

Initially, Gyowon had told Hyonae, *Neighbors are for exactly these types of emergencies, of course fellow moms would know how you feel, so please don't worry about Darim. We can take care of her while you help your mother-in-law.* If she were fully recovered from the fight, she would have made the offer more confidently. It wouldn't be easy, of course, but it wasn't like both parents would be gone; Sangnak could bring Darim over in the morning, then take her home after work. Sangnak would have to go visit for a day or two since it was his own mother undergoing surgery, but if push came to shove, Gyowon didn't have any issue with putting three kids to bed in her apartment. Things were still strained between her and Yeosan after all the drama in the middle of the night, and it had been somewhat awkward to continue seeing her neighbors as though nothing had happened, but life puttered along without waiting for Gyowon to recover. She was already forcing herself to maintain a sense of normalcy for the kids, so it wouldn't physically be a big lift.

But Hyonae had immediately refused her offer without even a smile. Honestly, even Gyowon would have declined a similar suggestion by a neighbor, saying she appreciated the sentiment. Even though their lives had become enmeshed, it would be difficult not to feel nervous about the arrangement. A grandmother would likely be better at soothing her own grandchild than a neighbor. Especially from a mom's perspective, it would be more reassuring to choose her own mother. If she were in Hyonae's position, she wouldn't have the energy to worry about her child while sleeping at an unfamiliar hospital and taking care of a patient. Gyowon could also understand any hesitation Hyonae might feel about leaving her child with a family that had fought at the top of their lungs not too long ago.

But Hyonae didn't seem to be declining her offer because she felt bad about being a burden or because she was nervous about leaving Darim with the neighbors—that much was clear. Niceties—*thank you so much but that won't be necessary*—weren't a part of Hyonae's vocabulary. In the network you formed when your child was born, and which strengthened through years of child-rearing, declining offers and expressing thanks were always deployed in tandem like a gift set. A well-timed smile acted as the bow on top. Hyonae's refusal showed her intention to deflect help from anyone else. This sentiment hadn't emerged from personal beliefs, or a strict adherence to privacy; instead it seemed she had assumed she would have to return the favor and take care of Seah and Ubin in a similar situation (regardless of how remote such a possibility might be). While it could be that Hyonae's predilection was a product of having the kind of efficient, restrained personality that didn't allow her to burden anyone else or rack up any debt for even the briefest time, it was clear that this wasn't the case if you observed Hyonae's life for even a second.

Sure, it depended on your personality, but it would be impossible to handle only your own affairs without sharing the burden in some way when one kid became two and then three and the kids all fell sick at different times. What was Hyonae planning to do when that inevitability happened? There would surely come a time when she wouldn't be able to go to the youngest's school performance because the eldest had an open house, when she wouldn't be able to pick up the middle one from an after-school program because the baby had to go to the doctor. Gyowon had always wondered how someone as individualistic as Hyonae had even thought to move into a communal living situation like this one. Hyonae paid hardly any attention during playtime with the kids, and she was sloppy in every possible way; how she managed to take care of her own daughter was a mystery. It was truly painful to face her every day when it was obvious she was participating in the co-op day care only because she had no other choice, her expression making it clear that if she could, she would leave instantly. While Gyowon completed all of her assigned duties like clockwork (except for the day she'd gone to the ER to get stitches), Hyonae showed up twenty or thirty minutes late nearly every day. It was hard to assign her even the simplest of tasks, like writing down the daily activity log, when she was so scattered.

In any case, because of all this, today there were only three kids, Siyul, Ubin, and Seah, and two adults, Gyowon and Euno. Things felt more relaxed since there were only half the usual number of kids. Euno had just suggested forgoing the day's nature-oriented program and heading to a big kids' café or somewhere in town.

"I wondered if the kids might feel a bit isolated because they're always in nature. Maybe it's time for them to jump on a trampoline and roll around on mats and throw themselves in a ball pit."

Might feel a bit isolated... To Gyowon, that sounded like he was speaking about her.

"If we call a taxi now, I think we can get back before everyone comes home. And it won't be too crowded on a weekday."

"That's not a bad idea, but wouldn't people think we're a couple with three kids?" asked Gyowon with a grin, and Euno cocked his head as if mulling it over, then shrugged.

"Who cares? We'll never see them again anyway, so they can assume whatever they want."

Once Euno locked in their plans, Gyowon felt the shadows that had darkened her nerves lifting. She sensed that today would be easy and fun, and it even felt like their hours with the kids were already over. Because there weren't as many kids, she didn't have to make soup in the big pot or set the table with the healthy vegetable banchan; they would eat lunch at the kids' café in town, then, on their way home, pick up pizza for dinner. They would revel in a greasy, unhealthy, high-calorie feast topped with cheese and thin rounds of potato and olives and bacon and more; feeding the kids pizza for once in their lives wouldn't kill them.

Honestly, Gyowon had been feeling disillusioned about all the tasks that had been given to her, all the tasks she had, for the most part, assigned herself, and all that resulted from these tasks. More often than not she felt that all the tasks and duties she'd been laboring over every second of every day meant nothing at all, and she thought that Yeosan and his family too often used cutting words to shoot her dead. Each time that happened, Gyowon distracted herself by approaching homemaking and child-rearing with an earnest desperation, memorializing the results of her efforts in a carousel of pictures and short videos that could be "liked" and admired by anyone.

You're so talented, coming up with such a great design on a budget. Where did you get the fabric?

I bet my husband would come home early if our place looked like this!

Did you take cooking classes? I can practically taste the food!

This is more than just a nice table setting and pretty plating and great pics. It looks like a professional made it! It must have taken hours.

Perfectly bite-sized for kids. Your feed makes this lazy mom feel bad for her kids!

Where did you buy the picture word cards and the felt Velcro set you used in the English lesson in your last post?

The praise from her followers quickly vanished as the feed refreshed, but for Gyowon, if it was going to go unpaid anyway, then making a record of her labor and attracting more eyeballs was a form of emotional compensation.

All of that was before they'd moved to their current home. Yeosan had changed jobs twice in the few years since Ubin was born, mostly because his pay was always late, a chronic issue when working for small-scale subcontractors. By the time Gyowon was pregnant with Seah, Yeosan had landed at the small company run by his family. He'd wanted to avoid working there if at all possible; the insinuation of *we're family, you know exactly how much money there is* frequently delayed his paychecks. Although he wasn't kept in the dark like at his former jobs and his pay-checks somehow, if irregularly, managed to hit their bank account before the next payday, none of that made much of a material difference to Gyowon as she struggled to make ends meet.

In such a situation, the only way to supply what the kids needed without going bankrupt was to make maximum use of the large resale sites specializing in children's gear. That in itself wasn't anything special, as most women with kids did that. It was common for moms to slather expensive hypoallergenic moisturizer on their children's bodies while they themselves made do with samples they collected as they walked through store aisles.

Newborn gear like a pump or a breastfeeding pillow were rented, and toys and books and clothes and shoes and strollers were bought secondhand. Online groups that catered to moms who were several levels wealthier would bulk purchase luxury baby carriers and tank-like strollers from overseas and buy toys crafted out of organic wood and cloth, posting picture after picture on community boards, and Gyowon bought those used goods for Ubin at the lowest price possible, haggling and negotiating, then stored them carefully for

Seah to use later. Kids grew so quickly that it was a no-brainer to buy them secondhand clothes. She did buy new socks and underwear since they wore out easily, their underwear quickly soiled with all manner of bodily excretions, but she didn't need to go out of her way even for those; a constant stream entered the house as holiday and birthday gifts from friends and family. For outerwear, she bought everything secondhand and washed them before the kids wore them. Since the kids would grow out of the clothes after a few wears, she wasn't bothered by fuzz or missing buttons as described by the seller; these were easily remedied by mending and taking care when washing them. After her kids grew out of them, she posted the clothes back on a reuse site and someone else would buy them from her, continuing the economic cycle. She was proud of her thrift even if nobody acknowledged it, and this pride propelled her through life. After all, even if her husband didn't bring home much money, she was capable of buying a luxurious British stroller that was known to protect the baby's spine, all for half the going rate.

It was important to carefully inspect the item and negotiate a reasonable price. The seller tended to want the best price possible, regardless of any scratches or the item's overall condition, while of course the buyer wanted to pay the lowest price. Gyowon stubbornly insisted on a refund if she discovered a flaw that hadn't been evident in the pictures (This book series was advertised as being so new that the spines would crack when you opened the books, but the corners came dented and torn. Someone's written their name in the back of a book, too. None of this was in the description, so I'll be returning this.), and when this happened, the sellers, who were other housewives stuck at home with their kids all day long, often found it burdensome to process a return and instead offered a steeper discount on the price or the delivery fee in an attempt to complete the transaction. Gyowon must have saved millions of won more by taking these steps; having gotten a taste for driving a bargain, she began negotiating hard, though in her mind she wasn't doing anything unusual, until she ended up on the receiving end of a pile-on.

It all began when a user posted a screenshot of Gyowon's message on a moms' group forum, obscuring only part of her user ID. Here's the cheapskate who wanted the BNWOB Magic Fan book series for 30K when I put it up for 70K (retail price 120K). I know we're all in the same boat with young kids and should give people grace, but this is ridiculous. To accompany that jeering post, the seller had uploaded a screenshot of the messages they'd exchanged.

DS loves Magic Fan but money's a little tight. Would you be willing to let it go for less?

What were you thinking? It's BNWOB and it's just been sitting there, but LO has grown out of this reading level. I'm already taking a hit at this price.

The lower the better! No worries if not possible.

What's your price?

I know you're asking for 70K incl delivery, but how's 30K w/ separate delivery fee? If that doesn't work for you, I could do 40K w/ separate delivery fee.

The screenshot ended there, and some moms in the comments seemed to feel sorry for Gyowon, saying, She must have been really hard up to throw out that number, but the majority found this behavior embarrassing, or raged that people like her were the reason everyone thought all moms were shameless. It's not like we buy things for the advertised price because we're rich, they commented. We're all on a tight budget. The screenshot of their exchange spread to other groups, even ending up on the home page of a portal site with the inflammatory title The Cheapskate Mom of Joonggonara Strikes Again.

While it was true that the retail price for the Magic Fan series was a hundred twenty thousand won, that was the retail price; Gyowon knew that they were being sold for around seventy thousand won, the price having been driven down by competition among small and medium-sized wholesalers. Which meant that the seller was trying to get the exact amount she'd paid, even though the books had already been opened and used. In Gyowon's mind, even a never-worn item of clothing was considered secondhand the moment it was taken out of its packaging. Even if people didn't know all that context, the part Gyowon wanted to rebut was the way the exchange was framed; while it was true they had messaged back and forth, it had continued beyond that screenshot.

I'm afraid that won't be possible. I was planning to sell this so I can buy another series. Sorry about that.

No worries at all. Have a nice day.

You too. Hope you find what you're looking for.

Gyowon hadn't clung persistently to something the seller said was impossible; she had opened negotiations with zero expectations, just trying to see if there was someone out there willing to come down to her price, and the exchange had ended pleasantly. How could the seller then turn around and stab her in the back like that without even blacking out her full user ID? Gyowon's ID soon became synonymous with shameless, irrational behavior, and other users piled on to share their own experiences with her.

Oh, I know her. She was the worst. Everyone knows that used things won't be in mint condition, but she sent so many messages saying the stain was bigger and more obvious than what was in the pics that I ended up refunding 10K. At first I offered to refund the 4K delivery fee but she insisted on returning it. How much would she have saved by acting like that? I bit the bullet because paying for delivery both ways would have been such a waste of time and brain space.

Does she still have little kids? I posted underwear that the kids never got to wear and she was like, it'll be touching my kid's bare bottom, how would I know it wasn't worn when the packaging is open, and asked if she could take it for free and pay only for the shipping fee. Yes, the packaging was open, but the tags were still on! It was obviously new. Who puts clothes on their kids with tags on? That was a really long time ago and I didn't bother replying. I can't believe she's still living like that.

After that incident, Gyowon became depressed; things hadn't improved much since then, but she'd given up on the idea of therapy or going to the doctor about it because of the astronomical cost. Her only joy in life was displaying her culinary skills or cute, unique interior decor ideas through pictures for people she didn't know; now that the kids in their communal apartment building had begun spending their days together, she'd taken on nearly all the cooking and felt more useful.

The years she spent buying things while being called cheap by anonymous people on the internet and the days she spent protecting what they had instantly became meaningless. She had no idea why she'd lived so tenaciously, gluing together all the gaps in her daily life, when there had been an entirely separate hole through which water was leaking out. A few months ago, Yeosan, who somehow used to bring home his full pay even if it was at odd intervals, had begun bringing home an envelope with just a few ten thousand won bills in it, and only when she nagged him about money. Recently Gyowon had called her sister-in-law to gripe about how impossible it was to make ends meet with what felt like an allowance. What she learned during that conversation was that the company had gone bankrupt, her sister-in-law's husband had taken huge amounts of company funds before getting caught and sent to jail, and in an attempt to fix it, Yeosan had been running around, giving his sister every little bit of his own salary—and the entire family had kept this news from Gyowon the whole time.

"Wouldn't that make you hit the roof? I have no idea how they thought they could hide it from me, when it's obvious how much money comes in. Basically the whole family colluded against me and decided I could be fooled." Gyowon's eyes tracked the kids as they boisterously went up and down the inflated slide.

Euno hesitated, not sure how to respond. Her voice was low, her expression indifferent, as if she were talking about someone else. He wasn't in a position to offer even the most perfunctory of consolations, as he himself received a paltry sum every month from his wife, and he'd kept himself afloat for years by working for a day here and a day there on film shoots until he found himself in the situation he was in now, all but ready to give up on filmmaking.

"Sorry," Gyowon said. "We're on a rare outing, and here I am, being a downer."

"No, not at all. Please don't say that." Euno decided that, with nothing else to offer, his role was to listen attentively. "I know this is difficult to talk about. I'm here to listen. Don't worry about it. You can tell me anything you want, and that way you'll be able to show a happy face to the kids."

"Thank you. I'm done, though. I just feel like I'll have to make a decision at some point. And it gets more complicated when I think about all our loans and the kids. The whole thing is a huge headache."

Noticing how Gyowon's cheeks drooped as she

flashed a bitter smile, Euno stood up. "Uh, well, do you want something to drink? I'll get… And something for the kids, too. Now, where's the…?"

"It's okay. I packed enough drinks, so I can take them out when the kids come over. Not yet." Gyowon tapped her backpack, still looking away from Euno.

Euno had been wondering why she hadn't opened the backpack, but then he glanced over at another table and saw a young staff member uncomfortably asking a group of women for their cooperation. "You can't bring outside food in here. Please put it away."

It appeared that the women had brought their kids to the kids' café, along with burgers and gimbap they'd bought elsewhere, and had been caught eating the contraband. A woman who seemed to be the leader of the group smiled at the employee. "We're almost done. Just a few more minutes? We'll clean up after ourselves. Could you look the other way, just this once?"

Euno tutted to himself. Whether they cleaned up after themselves wasn't the actual issue here, was it? The young employee sighed and gave them a half-hearted warning before leaving: "Well, please put it away quickly."

That employee would be the one to get in trouble if the owner or the manager came by. It was part of the social contract to buy the expensive, mediocre food they sold here when you visited, even if the portions were tiny and it wasn't something you actually wanted. This rule was reinforced by acrylic signs tacked up on the walls that said *No Outside Food Allowed*. But there were always people who didn't blink at this rule and nonchalantly brought food in, setting up a whole feast as if to rub their defiance in the employees' faces. Some people ignored the rules but considered their behavior to be a virtue of thrift. At least the moms at the next table over seemed to have enough awareness to understand that their behavior was embarrassing, ducking their heads and quickly finishing their food while sneaking glances at the employee, before shoving the aluminum foil and plastic waste in their bags. No matter where you went, there were always people who did precisely what they were told not to do.

But when it occurred to him that Gyowon had been planning to do exactly that, even if it was just drinks rather than a full meal, his face flushed. Judging from what he'd heard so far, it seemed that Gyowon was more than capable of doing that and then some. Euno couldn't begin to understand Gyowon's thought process since he wasn't interested in buying entire series of books, and Siyul seemed just fine reading whatever books they had at the public library. Whether the retail price was one hundred twenty thousand or seventy thousand won, Gyowon's decision to open with a thirty thousand won offer was beyond Euno's realm of comprehension. Were there really so many people who were irrational about so many small things in life, claiming it was for their children, that they ended up not feeling any shame?

That was when Euno concluded that he would pay for their whole outing, including beverages for everyone. Gyowon should be able to experience just how energizing and exciting it was to be on the receiving end of a generous gesture, how satisfying it was to spend money on herself or to receive something that was for her alone. More crucially, he had the foreboding sense that if he entrusted her with the purchase of the pizza, she would choose a buy-one-get-one-free promotion that would consist of basic, unappetizing pies and try to negotiate with the restaurant for a lower price by suggesting they remove a specific kind of cheese or by taking issue with some topping or other. She might even demand an extra side that wasn't part of the deal.

The plan was for Yojin to carpool home with Jaegang this evening. As Yojin worked on Saturdays, she was to drop Jaegang off in Seoul tomorrow morning, at a subway station that would be convenient for him to get to Danhui's family home. Then Danhui and Jaegang and the boys would drive home on Sunday night.

But long after their lunch break was over, having grappled with the decision, Yojin asked her cousin if she could leave two hours earlier than usual. She'd ended up asking late in the day because she had been trying to come up with a good excuse as to why she had to leave early, but her cousin didn't ask any follow-up questions; she just sounded a little annoyed, telling Yojin she should have mentioned it earlier.

Fewer patients came in the late evening since only a few practices in the medical building were open that late, and usually only on Thursday nights. Still, it could be that her cousin didn't really need Yojin anymore. Yojin had been working there for four years but the pharmacy had been in this location for eight. Occasionally her cousin would mention how difficult it was to pay the precipitously rising rent, and Yojin had noticed a few signs pointing to her irrelevance. The main clientele at her cousin's pharmacy were patients who didn't want to wait at the bustling pharmacy in the medical building, which meant they only saw middling profits, and for that, her cousin would complain, the premium she paid to be next to a medical building was too high. Soon, the surrounding commercial district would be redeveloped, with a bigger, newer medical tower planned for the next block over. The rumor was that half the practices in the medical building next door were planning to move into the new one, which would significantly impact both pharmacies and the building itself.

This was the context behind her cousin mentioning from time to time that running a smaller-scale neighborhood pharmacy would be less stressful, even if it was less profitable. She had once said to Yojin, *You should go work somewhere with an easier commute. You must barely be breaking even, with all that time and gas you're wasting by driving so far.* At the time Yojin merely thought her cousin was apologizing for not being able to give her a decent raise in three years, especially considering that she was still practically paid minimum wage, but when she thought back to that conversation, she realized her cousin might have plans to close down the current iteration of the pharmacy. Yojin realized she had been naive—as there would always be people who were sick and many practices would remain in the medical building next door regardless of the new tower's size, she'd assumed it wouldn't be a drastic hit to the bottom line even with customers leaving—and it also struck her that she and Euno were never destined to make serious money when they both lived their lives thinking on such a small scale.

Whichever way the pharmacy's fate went, Yojin was in a position to be let go at any moment. Right now, though, that wasn't her priority; she needed to escape the current situation she faced. She didn't care where the chips might fall. Any concerns about the fallout among these people, with whom she only had an ankle-deep relationship, crumpled like a thin sheet of paper, which she tossed away. She didn't have a good explanation for her unexpected behavior toward her neighbors, either. She hated that, even at this very moment, she was worrying about what others might think, even briefly. She found herself thinking that everything at home, from the banchan to the pots to the dining table to the toys to the learning materials, was stewing with contempt for her.

Yojin didn't care if Jaegang had to hitchhike home that night or had to take out a high-interest emergency loan to pay for a taxi—or whether he made it home at all. She would turn off her notifications and silence her phone and ignore his calls, and if he trekked all the way to the pharmacy and learned she wasn't there, he would surely conceal his befuddlement and head straight to Danhui's parents', not showing his confusion over why his plans had abruptly shifted. He could pretend to be the good dad, the earnest son-in-law who arrived a day earlier than expected to maximize his time with Danhui's family. Yojin needn't concern herself with what might happen.

She had gone back and forth for days before pulling the trigger on the voice recorder, but it would take a few days for it to arrive; this morning, Jaegang's words and behavior on their way to work had finally crossed the line Yojin held with a smile. Of course he didn't curse her out or say anything awful, and she would have to consider what he said to her as mostly praise; this was what made Yojin hesitate before making her decision.

"One of my clients bought this from Duty Free on their way home from a trip abroad. Why don't you take it? It made me think of you. It matches your skin tone perfectly."

"Me? No, no. Give it to Danhui-ssi. Why would you give it to me?"

"Danhui would need a shade darker than this, and she has a particular brand she uses. She's picky about these things."

"I appreciate the thought, but I don't think I should take it. I do need something that covers up blemishes, but this looks expensive."

"Just think of it as a free gift or a sample from a store. I got it as a gift myself. Not that I've ever noticed you having blemishes or any skin problems. And you have good style. Very pretty, like I've said before."

Yojin quickly deflected the compliment, to make it clear that she wouldn't allow him to encroach on her self-esteem. "What style? Of course not. I throw on whatever since I just work at a pharmacy. And..."

Then again, it was true that Yojin had barely any blemishes or other skin trouble compared to mothers her age, steeped as they were in chronic exhaustion from child-rearing and housework. She didn't do anything special to maintain her complexion. She had also been born with a slim body type and fast metabolism, but she often wondered if her looks were the pinnacle of what she'd been allotted in life. This so-called advantage, this useless blessing that hadn't even helped her find a decent job, would start to leach away around forty anyway. At best, the fact that she didn't need to spend a lot of money to adorn herself with makeup and various other cosmetic services was the only useful aspect about her looks.

Back when Yojin took any temp job she could find, her looks helped her get noticed. She'd get work as a member of the studio audience for an educational TV program or an extra in a movie, and once someone had even screenshot a close-up of her and posted it online, but she quit after a half dozen gigs, having figured out that her height and looks were middling at best and wouldn't carry her any further. Now all she had was her life with Euno, whose career was in shambles, and the sparkling presence that was Siyul. She hung on, aware that her life hadn't fully gone off the rails because she at least had her daughter, but it was in fact impossible for the three of them to live off Yojin's pharmacy job. Yojin had been plugging the holes by dipping into bank accounts her grandfather had unexpectedly left her when he died.

Euno, who spent lots of time around actors on set, barely noticed when he walked by beautiful women on the street, even during their short courtship. It had been years since he'd told Yojin she was pretty, especially after Siyul was born and she was drained from work and childcare. Maybe that was the reason Jaegang's words landed in Yojin's ears in an unfamiliar way, words that patched together the remnants of her self-esteem. That was partly why Yojin didn't initially feel much aversion to his comments.

"...well, thank you," said Yojin. "I feel like I owe

you one. I won't be able to reciprocate with something this nice, but maybe a meal at some point."

"How's tonight?"

"Sorry?" The wheel under Yojin's hands shook. "Oh, I mean, we should get our families together...us and Danhui-ssi and the kids...next time. But maybe that's not very inclusive of the others."

"Right, it would be a little awkward to throw a party for no reason. Tonight's perfect, since Danhui's at her parents' with the kids. You'll be done at the usual time?"

"Tonight? Well, it's so sudden and..."

"Don't worry. It's on me."

"On you? That makes even less sense. The whole reason for it was..." She had been trying to express her gratitude, but Jaegang's offer to buy dinner muddied things. It didn't seem right to go out, just the two of them. His phrasing suggested something secret, a covert intention of some sort... To put it in the worst light, a coercive streak seemed to rip through the cover of kindness and familiarity. Yojin's heart began to race.

"Isn't it reason enough that I want to buy you dinner? We've been carpooling together all this time without ever sitting down for a nice, intimate meal together. I'm glad we're finally doing that."

Why did they need intimacy to begin with? Had he relied on the familiar and reassuring activities of daily life, using gifts of cosmetics and brunch as props, to wear her down, to try to disarm her?

"So it's a date," Jaegang concluded. "It's not a big deal. We're just grabbing dinner before we head home. You have a family waiting for you. It's not like we have time to do anything more than that anyway."

Anything more than that.

The suggestion was that if she didn't have people waiting for her, if Euno and Siyul were out of town, then he wouldn't hold back. The insinuation roiled Yojin's gut. Now that she thought about it, his banter had long gone beyond neighborly jokes; it had just taken her a while to see it.

"Well, we can talk about that later. I'm going to concentrate on driving."

"But we're here."

Only then did she realize that they'd pulled up in front of Jaegang's office; she stamped on the brakes. She lurched forward and flopped back into her seat.

"I'll text you later. Think about what you want to

eat." Jaegang grinned as usual and walked lightly into his building.

Yojin stared at him in a daze before belatedly shaking her head. *Wait, no, you can't keep making something out of nothing...* She glanced at the clock and realized the pharmacy would be opening soon; the roads must have been more congested today. She didn't have time to run after him. And, anyway, even if she rushed into his office and sternly told him that they shouldn't have a meal together and it was inappropriate for them to spend time alone, she'd be the one they'd say caused a scene, the one who'd be judged by the army of suits as they marched past. She slowly raised her foot off the brake and realized that her palms, gripping the wheel, were slick with sweat.

What spurred Yojin to finally act was her discovery that the foundation he'd given her wasn't sold in Incheon Airport's duty-free shops. It was actually a limited-edition exclusive from a curated selection of luxury brands inside a department store—she learned this by searching online during a lull at work.

She wondered if she should take a picture of it and

send it to Danhui, explaining what had happened and getting her involved, but even if she confided in Danhui, why would Danhui take Yojin's side over her own husband's? Even assuming Danhui found it strange enough that she raised it with him, Jaegang seemed entirely capable of inventing any number of explanations that cast him in a favorable light. Her male neighbors would look at her askance and deem her an oversensitive troublemaker, while the women would either think she was incredibly odd or that she flirted with someone else's husband—her reputation would be sealed from then on, frozen like taxidermy.

Despite all that, Yojin remained considerate and sent Jaegang a final message so he wouldn't come all the way to the pharmacy after she'd already left.

Instead of coming to the pharmacy, I think it would be best if you went straight to your in-laws' for the weekend. Let's consider your offer of a meal never happened. It makes me uncomfortable and I don't think it's respectful to Danhui-ssi, either. I'll give you back the duty-free item, I mean the limited-edition foundation. I hope this doesn't offend you.

Yojin silenced her phone and turned off the vibration, placed it face down, and left it there without checking the barrage of KakaoTalk messages coming in from Jaegang.

She wanted to put an end to things cleanly and planned to return the gift in private, but she knew she had to tell Euno about what had happened in case Danhui found out somehow or Jaegang made things up to cover his tracks. If Yojin was in Euno's shoes and found out belatedly about a conflict brewing with the neighbors, she would definitely feel betrayed; regardless of what the situation was, she was sure he would feel bitter about being blindsided by something like this. If Yojin beat them to it and confided in Euno, he might react matter-of-factly and say, *Really? What a weird guy. Why is he sniffing around a married woman? Let's do our best to stay away from them. I'll keep an eye out, too,* and leave it at that, but the later he found out, the more likely it was for the accusatory arrow to swing toward Yojin: *Why did you let the problem get bigger and not say anything? You actually liked the attention, didn't you?* Yojin didn't even want to consider that exhausting possibility, no matter how confident she was in her ability to prove her innocence.

Yojin stepped on the gas. She'd tell Euno everything today while Danhui and her husband were away. Some might think that leaving work early just to avoid having dinner with someone was an overreaction, and it would have been more reasonable to text Jaegang and make him promise to stop. But when she remembered how Jaegang had come all the way to the pharmacy the other day, it seemed entirely within the realm of possibility for him to ignore her wishes and come over, catch her off guard, and consider that to be a wonderful surprise.

As she neared the village, the stench of manure from some farm or other wafted into the car. Yojin rolled up the windows and held her breath. The miniature air freshener she kept in the car emitted a delicate floral scent that struggled to mask the odor, and the two opposing smells mingled to create an even more awful, strange stink. Those forceful particles pushed away any positive thoughts and filled the space with the reek of organic matter.

When they first received the application for the communal apartments, they had been told that no animal pens or factories or garbage dumps were located within five kilometers; it bothered Yojin that she frequently smelled this terrible stench. Normally they didn't notice it when they were at home, and Euno and Siyul said they smelled it only when they'd gone on an outing deep in the valley, meaning that this stench must be a nuisance only for the people commuting in and out of the village. Now each time Yojin smelled the manure she found it hard to breathe. Then her head would grow heavy with the weight of her daily life and the challenge of maintaining all its parts. Even though it was just the smell of livestock wafting over, even though it was natural for cows and pigs and any other living being to expel waste, Yojin was weighed down by an all-encompassing torpor that accompanied the thought that everything around her—the golden fields, the still-green leaves dangling on trees, the full, low-hanging clouds—was a mere scene printed on photosensitive paper, and that this invisible stench was the only real thing that endured.

Before she could fully escape the odor's sphere of influence, her old car, which had been finicky of late, began to rattle. Worried, Yojin pulled the car as far off the road as she could and listened closely. The engine's gurgles were growing dire; she decided to turn off the car and wait about five minutes. When she tried starting the engine again, nothing happened.

The car had broken down.

She called the insurance company, only to hear that they didn't have anyone nearby; someone would get to her in about two hours. The sun would have set by then; it would be nighttime. She didn't expect they would drop everything and rush over to the countryside for a small car when their premiums were very low. What a terrible stroke of luck. She was only a kilometer away from home. After agreeing to an appointment time, Yojin told the agent that she'd go home to wait, not really believing that someone would actually arrive on time. She'd pulled her car far enough onto the shoulder that anyone who drove by could pass it. Even though home was only a kilometer away, Yojin kept glancing back as though someone were chasing her. She nervously hustled along, and the stench that had settled in her nose slowly began to vanish.

Yojin was relieved when she reached the entrance to the apartment building. She also sensed an unfamiliar energy, maybe because she rarely came home this early. What were the kids doing that it was so quiet? Of course, three of the kids were away today and it was the time of day when everyone was in their own homes, having dinner or playing, but she always heard a kid or two crying or throwing a tantrum whenever she pulled into a parking space. Yojin found herself smiling. Even though she wasn't home early for a happy reason, she could imagine how thrilled Euno and Siyul would be to see her. Would they be surprised? They must be eating dinner. She felt herself relax as she became aware of her hunger. She didn't need anything fancy; all she wanted was kimchi and a fried egg on rice and a drop each of sesame oil and soy sauce to season the whole thing. How many instant rice packets did they still have at home?

That was when she heard laughter, rolling and bursting like ripe pomegranate seeds, drifting toward her with the breeze. A low, full voice punctuated the laughter. Yojin silently approached the noise. They must be at the outdoor table, she thought. It was getting colder, so it seemed odd to eat dinner outside. She was eager to fill Euno in on what had happened, but she figured she'd venture to the outdoor table first. If Sangnak or Yeosan were already out there, she'd say hello and smile as if nothing were wrong, spare Siyul any worry. Yojin slowed down as she drew near. She could smell the warm, rich scent of cheese and roasted vegetables and meat. Although Gyowon had been struggling lately, she must have cooked up quite a feast for the smaller group tonight. Was it... pasta? Pizza? None of them had an oven. Did they go buy frozen pizza and microwave it? It seemed out of character for Gyowon to heat up prepared food when she insisted on organic homemade food as much as Danhui.

Words intermittently landed in Yojin's ears and fell away. Euno was talking more and more in between Gyowon's peals of laughter. *Nouvelle blah blah blah... Jean-Luc Godard and François Truffaut...the May 1968 protests and blah blah turning point...* Now Euno was just listing names like Hou Hsiao-Hsien and Edward Yang. By the time Yojin thought, *How in the world is this man able to drone on about his sole interest to our stay-at-home-mom neighbor? Is he rambling like that because people are sitting around and giving him endless encouragement?* she found Euno and Gyowon sitting side by side at the communal table.

"Oh, you're home so early!" Euno said. "What's the occasion?"

"Yojin-ssi, you're home! If we'd known, we would have ordered more food."

Were the other two men still at work? Only Euno and Gyowon were at the table.

"Have a seat," Gyowon said. "You haven't eaten yet, have you? There's more upstairs. We can go up together in a second."

Of course they would have to sit close by, since it would be awkward if they were too far apart, but they were side by side, not across from each other, near the take-out pizza box containing a few slices of thin-crust pizza.

It was a large table made for a big family, but they were sitting shoulder to shoulder. She figured it would have been easier to share the pizza like that, and sure, they'd gotten take-out pizza, which was not a problem, either. Yojin often longed to just serve Siyul delivery food, and she'd ordered in frequently before moving out here. Plus, Yojin wasn't home during the day, so she didn't feel she had the standing to criticize them over what they fed the kids or how they spent their day; she didn't care if the pizza cheese was organic.

But—

"Where are the kids when the two of you are out here?" This was the only question Yojin was interested in. Was Siyul watching the younger kids on her own?

Euno replied breezily, "Oh, Seah's sleeping and Siyul and Ubin are eating dinner in Gyowon-ssi's kitchen. We asked them if they wanted to come out here for dinner, but they said no, they wanted to stay in."

It was ludicrous for the two adults to be out here without the kids, so much so that she couldn't bring herself to ask, *What is Siyul supposed to do if Ubin acts out again or tips so far back in his chair with pizza in his mouth that he falls and hits his head on the floor? Are the other dads upstairs with them?* Yojin ignored her husband and looked straight at Gyowon.

"But the kids are together only until early evening, right? When did they start eating dinner together?"

Euno cut in again as if defending Gyowon. "Oh, just tonight, as a special treat. Since the other kids and moms weren't here today, we called a taxi and went to the kids' café in town. They all had a great time."

Of course a field trip was something they could go on, and it would have been thrilling for the kids to break out of their daily routine. The round trip in a taxi would have cost less than a trip to and from Seoul. But Yojin didn't remember the group agreeing that they could dip into the funds, which all the families had pooled together, for a trip with only half the kids.

"We have receipts for everything, including the taxi," Gyowon said, perhaps having read Yojin's expression. "When the others come back, we'll balance the books and show them how we used the funds. Including the dinner we're having right now. We're going to make it really clear."

Euno waved her explanations away. "No way, that's out of the question. I'm the one who suggested the outing, so it's all on me today."

"But you charged too much on your credit card today, paying for the taxi and the entrance fees and the pizza. I don't think that's right when Yojin-ssi didn't agree to this beforehand. When Danhui-ssi comes back, we'll talk about it and I'll pay you back. Even if it's not for the whole day. To cover our portion."

Yojin obtained a lot of information in that short conversation. So that's what happened? He paid for everything? It occurred to her that all the notifications from the credit card purchases would be stacked up in her cell phone, which she'd kept silent all day to avoid Jaegang's messages. She'd used her phone only to call the insurance company.

"Well...we can talk about that later." Yojin watched a bundle of napkins flutter in the breeze and fly off the table. "I'm going up to check on the kids."

Gyowon stood to collect the napkins. "Sure. I'll clean this up and be right there. Go on up. Our front door code is..."

Yojin suppressed the thought that she didn't want to know Gyowon's front door code for any reason as she quickly turned away to head up the stairs.

Yojin punched in the six-digit code she'd managed to remember and opened the door. Seah was snoring on a mat in the living room, having kicked off half the blanket, and Ubin was sitting at the table, rocking his chair precariously back and forth, just as she'd imagined. He wasn't eating but instead gripping miniature cars in both greasy hands, racing them around the table he was treating as a racetrack. A few half-eaten slices of pizza remained in the cardboard box, along with a car on its hood, looking horrifically like a real car that had gotten into a major accident.

Yojin knew she should make him stop before he fell, but first, she looked around for Siyul and found her hunched over, resting her head on the coffee table in the living room. She must have already finished eating.

"Siyul."

Siyul looked up when she heard her mom's voice and sprang up to grab her. "Eomma, let's go. I want to go home."

That short, desperate request told Yojin everything she needed to know about the dinner.

"All right, let's go. Let's get you to bed. I'm sorry." Yojin wasn't sure what she was apologizing for, but her throat closed up as she spoke. She gathered Siyul in her arms, the child rubbing her tired eyes, and went over to Ubin.

"Ubin, Ajumma's leaving. Be careful, okay?"

Yojin didn't wait for Ubin's response and went to the front door, stuffing her feet into her shoes. The verbal warning was the bare minimum of her duty as an adult; she was holding Siyul and couldn't set up

Ubin in a safer spot on the floor. Yojin opened the front door and ran promptly into Euno.

"Oh, hey. Let's go. I came to get you. I can carry her."

Was Gyowon taking a long time to clean up, or did she suggest to Euno that Yojin seemed annoyed and he should go upstairs?

"It's fine. Move." But faced with the reality of not having enough hands, Yojin sighed. "If you want to be useful, you can go grab her shoes and jacket."

She brushed icily past Euno, who stepped aside, taken aback by his wife's anger.

Yojin carefully lowered Siyul onto her bed, and Siyul murmured something, her eyes still closed, before falling back asleep. The front door opened and she heard Euno placing Siyul's jacket on the coffee table.

"Is she sleeping?" he asked, standing behind Yojin like a relief carving on a wall.

Yojin nodded without looking at him.

"What happened today? You got home so early. Weren't you supposed to drive back with Jaegang-ssi?"

Although she'd come home early to tell him about Jaegang, she suddenly couldn't form a single thought.

When she didn't answer, Euno hesitated. "Did something happen today? I mean, what would have happened at the pharmacy other than having to deal with rude customers? Why were you being so snippy in front of Gyowon-ssi? That was embarrassing."

Yojin finally turned to look at Euno. "Looked like you were having a great time talking to Gyowon-ssi."

Euno let out a disbelieving laugh. "What? Are you jealous? You're not serious. Look, Gyowon-ssi said she was in a film club in college, so we started talking about films and it turns out we have a lot of interests in common. And I lost track of time. Between us, I can't believe you'd honestly be even a little bit jealous of her. I mean, look at the size of her."

What Yojin was feeling wasn't jealousy or anything remotely approaching it. Sure, she had felt a little excluded when she came upon them in the backyard, when she heard them mentioning names and titles unfamiliar to her. But to be fair, Euno had done most of the talking; he'd gotten excited that a woman was sitting in front of him, listening attentively and laughing along. And even though she knew that he made that mean-spirited comment to reassure her, Yojin was enraged that he was disparaging Gyowon's appearance when their neighbor had been listening patiently to his long-winded lecture just moments ago.

"My point is, how could you have a great time when you left Siyul to her own devices like that?"

"Like what? Seems like the kids were doing fine."

"Did you observe that yourself? Did you check on them to make sure they were fine?"

"We didn't hear anyone crying, and Siyul's a big girl. What's the big deal? We don't have to sit right next to her and watch her every move."

"No, we don't have to watch Siyul like that. But what about the other kids? They're little. Who knows what they'll get into? You really think Seah didn't wake up, not even once? You really think Siyul didn't have to go over and pull the blanket over her or pick her up to help her get back down?"

"We can ask her about that later. What's with you today? You know you can't just draw the line at someone else's kids when we're living communally like this. And Siyul's the oldest, so she's fully capable of helping out a little. What's so wrong about that?"

The thin filament illuminating the rational side of her mind finally snapped. "I'm going to my dad's for a while. With Siyul."

"What are you talking about?"

That idea had popped out of her mouth unexpectedly, but Yojin could feel her words bolstering the plan as she spoke with surprising conviction. "I'll be going to work from there. I'm going to look into a kindergarten near there, too. The elementary school isn't far from his place."

Euno shook his head disbelievingly. He clearly hadn't detected the despair shadowing her face. "What exactly is the problem here? Doesn't what I think matter, too? Why did we move here if you're going to be like this? Don't you remember? You're the one who wanted to apply to live here."

It was true—Yojin had been the one to find the announcement, the one to gather the application materials despite her assumption that they wouldn't get in. Euno had never cared to figure out what to do about housing, and his parents had thrown up their hands when it came to their creative son, who spent his days agonizing over screenplays, fated to be ignorant about the logistics of real life. Yojin, on the other hand, had been laser-focused on finding a place to live. She didn't stop to wonder whether they would be able to fulfill their end of the bargain by having three kids and living happily ever after—she just needed a place for their little family to live without constantly worrying about the next step. She'd applied to live here as a last resort to solve their housing issues, unable to rely on Euno to do anything as he agonized over his failed screenplay. Now Euno was putting the blame squarely on her.

"It's not like going into the shower with one thought and coming out with another. Now that we're here, we can't leave that easily. Have you figured out how much we'd have to pay back? Or are you just leaving with Siyul and telling me I'm supposed to stay here by myself?"

Yojin gnawed on the inside of her lip. She had no other choice, even if people might consider her decision naive or crazy. *It's not like you'd know how much we'd have to pay back anyway*, she thought.

"I don't know what set you off, but you need to cool down," Euno continued. "Of course it was awkward for me here, too, at first. I can get along with people on a set, but you know I'm not good with people in real life. Still, I've tried to get along with everyone here for Siyul's sake. Of course it's hard to live with people you don't necessarily click with. Did you think we'd be singing and skipping every day? We have to compromise and make concessions to live with others. Why are you acting like a child? We made this decision knowing that Siyul might have a little more on her plate because she's older. We can't go back on it now. It'll look like we're irresponsible. How can you just give up like that?"

Yojin had never imagined that words like *compromise* and *concessions*, words that implied social flexibility, would flow so naturally out of Euno's mouth, but perhaps that was the essence of communal living. And to Yojin his argument, though rational, felt infected, a swelling cyst. "Whatever. I'm going to stay there for a little bit. Just leave me alone. Like you said, I need to cool down."

She didn't bother mentioning that he was the real reason they'd joined this communal apartment building, that she'd had no choice but to apply because he'd been fundamentally uninterested in making money or raising a child. There was no use now in assigning blame.

"Okay, but do you have to cool down at your father's? He'll worry about us. What will we tell our neighbors here? How am I supposed to explain why you're acting like this?"

"Then should I go to your parents'?"

Euno shrugged and shook his head. "I give up. Do what you want. Let's see if you say the same thing tomorrow morning, when Siyul's awake." He snatched his jacket off the chair and went out the door, grumbling venomously, "It's impossible to talk to you when you're like this. I'm doing my best here." Then, unable to calm down, he snapped, "Is this because I used the credit card? Are you flexing because you're the one bringing in the money?"

Yojin didn't answer. Bringing in the money... What kind of flex would that be, when it was such a paltry amount? Was it his excessive spending today, despite their living paycheck to paycheck, that finally broke her? She'd be lying if she said it hadn't affected her, but was it fair to say that something so stingy and childish was the fundamental reason for their fight?

"Unbelievable," Euno snapped. "Don't worry. I'll pay you back for the whole thing." Having come to his own conclusions, he stalked off, the front door closing behind him before Yojin could make sense of her confused thoughts and explain herself.

Yojin grabbed a suitcase before she could change her mind and rifled through the drawers, throwing Siyul's clothes and belongings on the floor. She felt bad for Siyul but she'd carry her downstairs and put her in the car... which wasn't here. She'd have to call a taxi. She counted the cash in her wallet, then checked her cell phone to see how much she could spend before maxing out their credit card this month. Would she be able to afford a taxi ride all the way to Seoul? How much would she be able to borrow from her father? How much did she have left in the accounts her grandfather left her? She pushed away all these concerns; her only goal was to get away from this building, where the root of all her problems were. Jaegang might be back in a few hours. It was more likely that he'd gone to Danhui's parents' after she'd left without him, but no doubt the situation would only escalate if he did show up at the apartment building.

She was pulling her clothes out of the dresser when she found a thick manila envelope. Surprised, she dropped it, spilling its contents on the floor.

They were the documents she'd gathered to gain entry to this place, letters notifying them that they had been chosen, materials they'd had to submit after they were accepted—because of the sensitive personal information contained within them, she'd been overwhelmed by the prospect of ripping each document into shreds before discarding them, and had relegated the envelope to the back of her closet. She should have gotten rid of it a long time ago instead of leaving it here. She sighed and flipped through the file, and a stiff sheet of paper, perhaps a duplicate, slipped out of the stack. A short paragraph, written in Yojin's hand, followed by her signature. In it she described their dedication to having three children, and included phrases about *a beautiful promise we are making together for the future* and *a choice we believe will enhance our child's character* and so on.

She tore up the sheet and threw the scraps of paper in the trash, before unzipping her suitcase and packing in earnest.

Yojin carried Siyul, who grumbled as she was awakened from a fitful sleep, and managed to pull her suitcase outside with one hand. The taxi was waiting for her, noise and exhaust pumping into the dark. She soothed Siyul and placed her in the car. Euno came up from behind.

"Is this really necessary?" he asked. "I really don't understand why you're doing this."

Yojin half expected him to demand a neutral party come determine who was right in this situation. But Yojin had never lived in a world that was so black-and-white. She'd never experienced a situation in which one side gained and the other side lost as a matter of course. Without bothering to answer him, Yojin hauled her suitcase into the trunk and got in the car.

Euno sighed. "Go on and get some sleep, then," he told her, his voice laced with irritation. "I'll call you. Don't just turn off your phone. Answer it if you don't want to make this into a bigger thing, okay?"

Half his words were cut off as Yojin slammed the door shut.

Only when they drove past her car, still stranded on the side of the road, did Yojin start to calm down, knowing that she was finally creating distance from the communal apartments. Once she felt physically safe, she remembered the unread messages on her phone. She spotted notifications about the charges Euno had racked up, but she no longer cared.

Jaegang had inundated her with KakaoTalk messages. She scrolled down, pausing on each message.

Did I do something? Did I say something to make you uncomfortable?

I really didn't think you'd stand me up.

You're not here at the pharmacy. Is this for real?

I didn't think you were like this.

Did it seem like I was coming on to you? I just said I'd buy you a meal. You humiliated me. Your cousin looked at me like I'm a stalker. This isn't right.

Fine, we'll talk on Monday.

But Yojin wouldn't be there on Monday. Jaegang would pretend nothing had happened, even if a small part of him felt guilty. Or, to slander Yojin, he would frame himself as the victim in an uncomfortable, embarrassing situation, where he was merely trying to be nice. Maybe he would tell Euno: *Euno-ssi, you know, on Friday, Yojin-ssi sent me a text and then left without me. Did something happen at home? I thought I'd buy her dinner because she's given me a ride so many times, but I think she took it the wrong way. I'm afraid she was offended. What should I do? I think I'll apologize when she comes home. So that there's no misunderstanding, especially since we're all living here together.* Jaegang's insinuation that he would keep the peace by apologizing because she was upset, even though he'd done nothing wrong, would layer over Gyowon's encounter with Yojin, giving credence to the idea that Yojin just couldn't adapt to communal living. And Yojin couldn't be sure that Euno would fully be on her side when all of this went down.

That was when she noticed the animal stench seeping in from somewhere, even though the night breeze should have pushed away most of the smell. Yojin's window was closed, but she clicked the button anyway, trying to block even the tiniest amount of air that might enter.

"Sorry, could you check if any windows are open?" she asked the driver.

The driver raised his window, which had been open a crack. "I'm sorry, ma'am. It got stinky on my way over, so I opened my window a little to air out the car and forgot about it."

"That's all right. I'm sure it'll go away once we're out of this area."

I'm sure it'll all go away, she thought to herself. The stench, the space that the stench was part of, maybe even this place ruled by the stench.

The bright, rhythmic sound of pebbles bouncing against the tires thrummed over Yojin. The clinking was irregular and uncertain, something nobody in the world would consider music. As the taxi drove cautiously through the darkness, relying on its high beams as it went down the unlit road, Yojin felt a sudden ease, as though she'd flung herself across a satin blanket.

The modern building was painted in muted yellow and lavender, making it look like a children's art museum in a small regional city. Afternoon sunlight spread out from the corner of the hallway that linked the units together. As soon as they parked, their daughter bounded out like they'd arrived at an amusement park, and her husband grabbed their daughter's jacket and bag and ran after her. The woman smiled with satisfaction as she watched the father-daughter pair. She was relieved; she had assumed the building would be gloomy and sterile, as she'd heard the government had constructed the structure on a budget.

It was so quiet, no sounds of life in any of the twelve

units. Then a door opened and a heavily pregnant woman waddled into the yard, holding a boy and a girl by the hand. The newcomer nodded at the pregnant woman and introduced herself, explaining that they were to move in soon and had come by to show their daughter their new home.

The pregnant woman's face lit up; she looked as though she might step forward excitedly for a hug, but since her hands weren't free, she glanced at each of her kids and instructed them to say hello. The newcomer smiled at the bowing kids and asked the pregnant woman about the other neighbors, only to hear that four units had originally been filled but that three families had already moved out, leaving the pregnant woman and her family as the only residents.

That wasn't what the newcomer had expected but she kept her expression neutral, waiting for the pregnant woman to continue. She couldn't begin to guess why the residents had left without staying even two years, when it was so hard getting into this place to begin with. Even if they hadn't managed to have a third child yet, they would have had plenty of time until the deadline. But everyone had their own private, unspoken issues, she thought, undaunted. There was still a full list of families who had won the lottery, and as long as the wait-listed folks didn't give up, the remaining ten units would be filled in six months to a year, no problem.

That must have been why the front yard was deserted. If all twelve units were filled, there wouldn't be enough parking spaces for all the cars. And wouldn't each household have to have two cars, since they were so far from the city? She had always had her own car, and the same was true now, eight months after she'd left her job. There weren't any buildings around but plenty of land; they wouldn't have to park right in front of the building, within the boundary of the lot. The pregnant woman told her that they had bought a second car, a used one, only a few months ago. They had managed with one vehicle until then, but with the third on the way, they had to go to the doctor frequently. The newcomer felt relieved upon hearing that; she nurtured a glimmering hope that if her new neighbor succeeded in having three children, it wouldn't be impossible for her, either. After the birth of her daughter, whom she had managed to conceive after two miscarriages only to suffer from nine months of complications, from fibroids to frequent premature contractions, the elders in the family were quietly hoping for a boy next. She had quit her job for that eventuality, thinking perhaps it would be easier to get pregnant if she lived somewhere with clean air, clean water, and no stress.

Her pregnant neighbor said she was six months along and smiled, crinkling her eyes, which had dark circles under them. She said she was more tired now because she was older but that she was used to it, since being pregnant was a recurring condition for her at this point. It seemed she meant it as a joke, but something about that description was grim. The newcomer herself had been told by the doctor after her second pregnancy loss that recurrent miscarriages would be a concern.

Hearing her daughter laughing in the second-floor hallway, the newcomer looked up. The pregnant woman asked how old the girl was; when the newcomer replied that she was six, her new neighbor said, as if to herself, "The same age as Siyul when she first got here."

"Who's Siyul?"

At this question, the pregnant woman, Seah's mom, told her all about the three families who had left for various reasons within six months of one another.

Darim's mom was a freelancer who worked from home. The newcomer herself remembered very clearly how she constantly fielded phone calls and had to work throughout her four-month maternity leave, with the only benefit being that she didn't have to go into the office. She sympathized with how shackled the freelancer must have felt. She didn't know much about Darim's mom's specific situation, but she knew enough to know that office workers with Sisyphean daily commutes glared bitterly at you if you said you worked from home. It sounded as though Darim's mom was familiar with such attitudes; her sister-in-law hassled her, asking her to come and go on a whim despite Darim's mom's busy schedule. *You can come over since you don't go into an office, right? You have flexibility, so you should be able to do this, right?* The newcomer was well aware of the weight of such words, the way responsibilities were assigned. In any case, after a period of not being able to work or make money, Darim's mom apparently tore up all the pictures she'd been drawing and threw them out into the yard, shouting, *Do you think having three kids is going to be easy!* and then took Darim and split from her husband. The husband moved out soon after, since he could no longer live there without his family.

How embarrassing to move out in that fashion,

when everyone had gotten to know one another, saying hello every morning and night! The newcomer found herself shaking her head, thinking she would never end things with her husband like that, if only because of the humiliation. Anyway, it seemed that Darim's mom was very proud of her work and had ambition. The newcomer thought back to the fundamental reason why this communal living project had launched, and wondered if Darim's mom's line of work hadn't been a great fit with the purpose of this place. After the newcomer quit her job and embarked on a deep meditation practice, she had come to the conclusion that having three kids meant that, in reality, one person had to stay home and focus on child-rearing. This reality became crystal clear once you had more than two children, regardless of how robust the social support structures were, and right now, as a nation, they weren't even transitioning toward better systems yet. It was only natural that living in these communal apartments would require the person who decided to stay home to relinquish their personal desires and vow to be fulfilled by child-rearing alone. Such a role wasn't something to be endured, but one that should be considered a joy, the driving force of one's life. The newcomer fully thought this through before deciding to quit her job, and she believed she wouldn't regret anything. Sure, she no longer had a career, but she'd have the bond she'd forge with her daughter, and that would be enough to fulfill her.

At the very least, she was confident that she'd be better equipped to handle things than Siyul's mom, who Seah's mom described next. That family seemed a little untraditional, with the husband taking care of the child while the wife went to work, leading the newcomer to assume that Siyul's mom had been the CEO of a small company or something similar, but she was shocked to learn that she was an hourly worker. Of course, it probably depended on what kind of hourly gig it was, but from what the newcomer had seen during the course of her own career, there wasn't a single hourly job in existence that could plausibly support three people, especially if the husband stayed home. Unless you also dabbled in real estate speculation or won the lottery. The newcomer assumed that there must have been a good reason for the man to send his wife out to work—maybe he'd been preparing for the civil service exam or was launching a business—but she was shocked to hear Seah's mom's explanation that he was a writer, of all things. Writing? That didn't get you rice or water or anything at all these days. A man with a family, brazenly going all in on writing instead of working two jobs if that was what was needed? She was sure that, among writers, too, the rich would be getting richer and the poor would be getting poorer, except for those extremely rare instances when a celebrity talked about a book on TV, spurring major sales. Seah's mom didn't specify whether he wrote poetry or fiction or something else, but whatever he wrote, it would have been difficult to make a living from it. Only in times of plenty could a couple be deluded into thinking that they got along swimmingly. The newcomer didn't even want to imagine what direction her marriage would have gone if her husband hadn't managed to successfully extend his contract at work after she quit her job. She didn't need to hear more about how, one night, Siyul's mom suddenly left with Siyul, never to return, and how the writer husband soon moved out as well, to feel their frustration and despair.

The last family to leave was Jeongmok's, who, according to Seah's mom, appeared to be the most put together and seemed like they would stay the longest. Both husband and wife were passionate and energetic, the husband had a great job, they drove a foreign car, and, judging from what they ate and how they decorated their unit, they'd seemed financially comfortable, with Jeongmok and his brother always decked out in recognizable brands, like Burberry or Tommy Hilfiger. From Seah's mom's descriptions, the newcomer could tell what criteria her new neighbor used to judge the other families.

Even though Seah's mom claimed to be hesitant to reveal another family's personal tribulations, she went on excitedly, perhaps knowing that she would never see these people again and the newcomer didn't know them. Siyul's mom was attractive, and Jeongmok's dad had come on to her in some fashion. Before her abrupt departure, Siyul's mom had hung a small shopping bag on Jeongmok's door. Inside was some kind of limited-edition cosmetic whose name Seah's mom stumbled over; the newcomer recognized the brand but didn't correct the other woman's imprecise French pronunciation. Apparently Siyul's mom texted Jeongmok's mom, saying, *Your husband gave me this as a gift and hit on me*; later, when Siyul's dad and Jeongmok's parents got together to discuss everything that had happened, Siyul's dad had been shocked, saying he'd had no clue, while Jeongmok's dad insisted strenuously that he was misunderstood, claiming that he hadn't intended to make Siyul's mom feel that way. Rather than trying to figure out what had happened, Jeongmok's mom grew enraged. She was humiliated that her husband's behavior had caused a neighbor to misunderstand his intentions. In the end, the matter hit a dead end as Siyul's mom refused to pick up any of the three's phone calls, let alone meet up to discuss what had happened.

Even though these were stories about strangers, or maybe precisely because they were about strangers, the newcomer listened with great interest, perplexed that such drama could unfold in so small a building. She scoffed to herself, thinking, *It's all the same wherever you live.*

Anyway, she became worried about Seah's mom, who had been standing this whole time with her two kids despite her enormously pregnant condition, and so the newcomer suggested they continue talking inside. Seah's mom told her there was a better spot and led the newcomer to the backyard.

At first glance, the backyard appeared larger than the front, and the newcomer found herself thinking that this area could be used for additional parking if they ran out of spaces in the front...but then she spotted the large wooden table. It was wide and sturdy, a table that seemed to be modeled after the one pictured in da Vinci's *The Last Supper*, long enough to seat thirteen people in a row. This table, which Seah's mom informed her had been installed here before any of the residents had moved in, took up a lot of precious space in the backyard, situated as it was smack-dab in the middle.

The newcomer wondered if a few men could pick it up and move it to allow for a car or two to be parked next to it, but she soon shook her head. It looked impossible to budge without the use of a crane, and, though she couldn't put her finger on exactly why she felt this way, it seemed to her that this space was meant to be filled by this table. This was a space ruled by a strict sense of what should be, rather than utility or reason. It would be nice to bring in a swing or a small slide the kids could play on. After all, there would be a lot of kids living here soon; even if every family moving in had only two kids, that would already make twenty-four. The newcomer could imagine all the neighbors bringing out a portable grill for a barbecue on a sunny day. All twenty-four adults wouldn't fit around the table even if they wanted to, but the table had a sturdy presence, as though it would outlast everyone in this building. A communal table that would stand here, rooted in place, unchanging, no matter how many families cycled through, a crystal of warmth and wholesomeness shared among the neighbors. She didn't know why she felt this way, but the newcomer was certain she could gaze at this table, morning and night, for many years to come.

She heard her daughter laughing. It sounded like she was bickering lightheartedly with her dad as he told her to be careful. There were still three weeks before their move-in day, which they'd chosen for its auspiciousness.

★★★★★

Gu Byeong-mo was born in 1976 in Seoul. She studied Korean language and literature at Kyung Hee University. She made her literary debut with the novel *Wizard Bakery* (2009). It became a bestseller in Korea and was translated into numerous languages. She has published more than twenty works of fiction and won notable literary prizes.

Chi-Young Kim is a literary translator and editor, who trained as a lawyer before taking up translation, initially as a hobby. A recipient of the Man Asian Literary Prize for her work on *Please Look After Mom* by Kyung-sook Shin, Chi-Young Kim has translated over a dozen books, including works by Ae-ran Kim, You-jeong Jeong, and Young-ha Kim, among others. She was born in Boston MA and is now based in Los Angeles CA.

Chi-Young Kim's translation of *Whale* by Cheon Myeong-kwan was shortlisted for the International Booker Prize 2023.